W9-DJG-663

MAY - - 2024

MARVEL STUDIOS
CHARACTER ENCYCLOPEDIA
UPDATED EDITION

Written by Adam Bray and Kelly Knox

CONTENTS

Welcome to a world of adventurers, warriors, sorcerers, spies, inventors, Guardians, and Avengers! Characters are ordered by the chronological release date of the movie or streaming series they first appear in. You can also find characters by using the index on pages 236–239.

KEY TO ACRONYMS IN DATA FILES

IM *Iron Man*
TIH *The Incredible Hulk*
IM2 *Iron Man 2*
T *Thor*
CA:TFA *Captain America: The First Avenger*
MTA *Marvel's The Avengers*
IM3 *Iron Man 3*
T:TDW *Thor: The Dark World*
CA:TWS *Captain America: The Winter Soldier*
GOTG *Guardians Of The Galaxy*
A:AOU *Avengers: Age Of Ultron*
AM *Ant-Man*
CA:CW *Captain America: Civil War*
DS *Doctor Strange*
GOTGV2 *Guardians Of The Galaxy Vol. 2*
T:R *Thor: Ragnarok*
BP *Black Panther*
A:IW *Avengers: Infinity War*
AMATW *Ant-Man And The Wasp*
CM *Captain Marvel*
A:E *Avengers: Endgame*
WV *WandaVision*
TFATWS *The Falcon And The Winter Soldier*
L *Loki*
BW *Black Widow*
SCATLOTTR *Shang-Chi And The Legend Of The Ten Rings*
E *Eternals*
H *Hawkeye*
DSITMOM *Doctor Strange In The Multiverse of Madness*
MM *Ms. Marvel*
T:LAT *Thor: Love And Thunder*
SH:AAL *She-Hulk: Attorney At Law*
BP:WF *Black Panther: Wakanda Forever*
AMATW:Q *Ant-Man And The Wasp: Quantumania*
GOTGV3 *Guardians Of The Galaxy Vol. 3*
TM *The Marvels*

TONY STARK
Iron Man

Billionaire Tony Stark creates his first metallic suit of armor to escape The Ten Rings terrorist group. Over the years, Tony continues to develop ever more advanced versions of his Iron Man armor. As a founding member of the Avengers, he's always ready to suit up and fight threats to humanity. The villain Thanos wipes out half of the life in the universe in a catastrophic event that becomes known as the Blip. Tony works with other brilliant scientific minds to travel back in time, making it possible to bring back everyone who was lost.

Helmet recedes via nanotech

SUIT UP
Iron Man's Mark LXXXV armor uses nanotechnology to store itself inside Tony's chest-mounted RT (Repulsor Tech). The RT is a powerful electromagnet. It instantly forms armor around him and is even capable of creating a "gauntlet" that briefly wields the Infinity Stones—powerful and much sought-after objects.

Detachable housing unit for nanoparticles

Repulsor beam embedded in palm

DARING RESCUE
Iron Man's repulsor technology easily penetrates the exterior of villain Ebony Maw's spacecraft. Iron Man races to rescue his allies Peter Parker and Doctor Strange.

Tony makes the only choice that can save the universe from Thanos—even if it means him sacrificing his own life.

Nanobots automatically repair surface damage

DATA FILE

AFFILIATION: Stark Industries, Avengers, Pepper Potts, Morgan Stark
KEY STRENGTHS: Scientific genius, wealth, creativity; as Iron Man: flight, strength, durability, missiles, repulsor beams
APPEARANCES: IM, IM2, MTA, IM3, A:AOU, CA:CW, A:IW, A:E

High-speed thrusters for flight

PEPPER POTTS

Stark Industries CEO

As Tony Stark's personal assistant, Pepper Potts brings order to Tony's life. She uncovers the treachery of his business partner, Obadiah Stane, and Tony makes her CEO of Stark Industries. She continues to manage everything while he is on Avengers missions. Pepper fights beside Iron Man in her own Rescue suit to bring down Thanos in the Battle of Earth.

OFF AND ON
Pepper and Tony fall in love, but his dangerous fixation on saving the world strains their relationship. They take a temporary break, but later reunite, marry, and have a daughter, Morgan, together.

Smart business attire

Watch is a present from Tony Stark

IN CHARGE
Making Pepper CEO is one of the best decisions Tony Stark ever made. Pepper acts decisively and always keeps a cool head during their constant crises.

Pepper is infected with the dangerously unstable Extremis treatment by villain Aldrich Killian. Extremis allows Pepper to survive a fiery crash and blast Killian using an Iron Man repulsor.

DATA FILE

AFFILIATION: Tony Stark, Stark Industries, Happy Hogan, Morgan Stark
KEY STRENGTHS: Resourcefulness, reliablilty, leadership; with the Rescue suit: flight, enhanced strength and durability, projectile weapons, repulsor beams
APPEARANCES: IM, IM2, MTA, IM3, A:IW, A:E

JAMES "RHODEY" RHODES

War Machine

War Machine is the code name used by James "Rhodey" Rhodes when he wears the armor suits designed by his good friend Tony Stark. Rhodey confiscates Tony's Mark II armor when his friend's irresponsible behavior gets out of hand, but Tony doesn't hold it against him. In fact, he upgrades the armor with all-new features. Rhodey becomes an invaluable member of the Avengers and aids in their efforts to stop Thanos.

Spinal support and mobility assistance

Power source

Wrist-mounted missiles

Repulsor jets in boots

IRON MEN
Rhodey is always there for Tony, both as a good listener and as War Machine. Together they fight off Justin Hammer's drones before battling vengeful engineer Ivan Vanko.

MAYDAY
A blast from Thanos's ship traps Rhodey, Rocket, and Hulk in rubble beneath the Avengers Compound. Rhodey escapes from his damaged suit before Scott Lang rescues them. Rhodey puts on a different set of armor before joining the Battle of Earth.

DATA FILE
AFFILIATION: U.S. Air Force, Tony Stark, Avengers
KEY STRENGTHS: Honor, duty, loyalty, military training, piloting; as War Machine: flight, strength, missiles, repulsor beams, sonic cannon
APPEARANCES: IM, IM2, IM3, A:AOU, CA:CW, A:IW, A:E

When the Avengers disagree about registering their super-powers under the new Sokovia Accords legislation, Rhodey is unsure which side to choose.

HAROLD "HAPPY" HOGAN

Loyal bodyguard

Happy Hogan is Tony Stark's driver and bodyguard. After years of faithful service, he is promoted, working for both Tony and Pepper Potts. Happy takes his job seriously, which leads him into the line of fire after investigating a suspicious figure, Eric Savin. After his recovery, Happy is entrusted with even greater responsibilities.

NEW NAME
Harold "Happy" Hogan earns his nickname because Tony Stark likes to tease him about his glum personality. Happy has a heart of gold, though, and considers Tony and Pepper his closest friends.

Strong and fit due to boxing training

Smartly tailored suit

TAKING THE LEAD
Happy is a man of action. When he learns that Tony's nemesis Ivan Vanko and rogue rival Justin Hammer are up to no good, he races to Hammer Industries with no hesitation.

DATA FILE
AFFILIATION: Stark Industries, Tony Stark, Pepper Potts, Morgan Stark
KEY STRENGTHS: Loyalty, boxing, security expert, professional driver
APPEARANCES: IM, IM2, IM3, A:E

Iron Man Mark V briefcase

Happy is implicitly trusted by both Tony and Pepper, who promotes him to Stark Industries Security Chief. He comforts their young daughter, Morgan, during Tony's funeral.

RAZA

Terrorist commander

Raza is the leader of The Ten Rings terrorist group that kidnaps Tony Stark in Afghanistan. He tries to force the captured Tony into building missiles for him, but Tony builds an Iron Man suit instead and escapes. Raza is secretly buying weapons from Tony's villainous business partner, Obadiah Stane, but unwisely tries to renegotiate the terms of the agreement with him.

Raza decides to use Tony's Iron Man armor as a bargaining tool with Obadiah Stane.

DATA FILE

AFFILIATION: The Ten Rings
KEY STRENGTHS: Terrorist resources, Stark Industries weapons
APPEARANCES: IM

WRECKAGE

Raza and his men discover the wrecked armor of Tony's Iron Man prototype in the desert. They bring it back to camp but are unable to reassemble it.

Hot coal

Houndstooth check scarf

RAZA'S WEAKNESS

Raza isn't the head of The Ten Rings—that's a shadowy figure known as the Mandarin. Raza is a well-educated lieutenant, rising through the ranks of the organization. His arrogance makes him blind to Tony Stark's escape plan.

Camouflage jacket

OBADIAH STANE

Iron Monger

After inventor Howard Stark's death, his business partner Obadiah Stane becomes CEO of Stark Industries. Obadiah hides his resentment of Howard's son, Tony, and his inherited fortune. Obadiah bases his Iron Monger suit on Tony's prototype armor. Obadiah's engineers build a much larger suit, but it has a fatal flaw: Iron Monger freezes over at low temperatures.

DATA FILE

AFFILIATION: Stark Industries
KEY STRENGTHS: Deception, Stark Industries resources; as Iron Monger: strength, flight, missile launcher
APPEARANCES: IM

Helmet and chestplates separate to reveal cockpit area

BETRAYAL
Pepper Potts discovers on Obadiah's computer that he has been plotting with the terrorist group known as The Ten Rings.

Satellite phone and voice distortion

UNBALANCED
The Iron Monger hull is composed of steel with limbs controlled by powerful servo-hydraulics. The design focuses on smart weapons and targeting sensors over navigation.

RT stolen from Tony's chest

Mighty arms can lift a car

PHIL COULSON

Agent and ally

Working at the heart of counterterrorism intelligence agency S.H.I.E.L.D., under Director Nick Fury, Agent Phil Coulson is one of the secret organization's best operatives. Coulson is both likable and humble, despite his considerable authority within S.H.I.E.L.D. He assists Fury in recruiting the Avengers and integrating them into the team.

Encrypted
S.H.I.E.L.D. earpiece

DATA FILE

AFFILIATION: S.H.I.E.L.D., Avengers, Nick Fury
KEY STRENGTHS: Loyalty, resourcefulness, devotion, steadfastness, dedication
APPEARANCES: IM, IM2, T, MTA, CM

SACRIFICE

Faithful to the end, Coulson gives his own life in an attempt to stop Loki's escape from the S.H.I.E.L.D. Helicarrier. Though unsuccessful, his sacrifice motivates the Avengers to work together.

MEETING A HERO

Phil Coulson is a big fan of Steve Rogers. He owns a set of original Captain America trading cards and even helps design Cap's new uniform. He is almost nervous when he first meets his hero.

Coulson is one of Nick Fury's best agents. He helps Fury manage Tony Stark, Thor, and Steve Rogers.

DR. HO YINSEN

Selfless surgeon

Dr. Ho Yinsen first met Tony Stark at a New Year's Eve party in Switzerland in 1999, though Tony doesn't remember. Yinsen is taken prisoner by The Ten Rings and saves Tony's life when his heart is injured by a bomb. He helps Tony escape, knowing he can never actually leave himself.

INSPIRING MAN

Yinsen hails from Gulmira, Afghanistan. Though he leads a humble life and loses everything, he devotes himself to doing good. Yinsen encourages Tony to be a better man.

Brilliant scientific mind

Tie maintains dignity in captivity

TRUE FRIEND

Yinsen helps Tony assemble his Iron Man prototype armor. When the computer operating system takes too long to upload, Yinsen creates a distraction to buy Tony more time.

DATA FILE

AFFILIATION: Tony Stark
KEY STRENGTHS: Skilled doctor, scientist, multilingual
APPEARANCES: IM, IM3

Tongs hold vessel of melted palladium

Yinsen has essential engineering skill, and builds parts for Tony's armor as well as a temporary electromagnet for his heart.

NICK FURY

Director of S.H.I.E.L.D.

Nick Fury is the gruff, no-nonsense director of S.H.I.E.L.D. and the founder of the Avengers Initiative. He fakes his own death to survive during the rise of the evil Hydra group within S.H.I.E.L.D. When Thanos extinguishes half of all life in the universe, Fury calls in Captain Marvel just before he disappears. After Fury returns from the Blip, he runs missions from orbit in the S.A.B.E.R. space station.

Eye patch covers blind eye

Bulletproof vest

TAKING THE LEAD

Nick Fury has a hands-on command style. He doesn't lead from an office. He prefers to be at a S.H.I.E.L.D. Helicarrier helm and interact with agents directly.

Nick Fury is the first to brief Steve Rogers when he awakes.

Holster strapped to leg

PROVIDING BACKUP

After S.H.I.E.L.D.'s collapse, Fury works from the shadows. Maria Hill monitors the Avengers, allowing Fury to step in when needed, such as when he helps evacuate civilians in Sokovia.

Signature long leather coat

DATA FILE

AFFILIATION: S.H.I.E.L.D., Avengers, Skrulls, S.A.B.E.R.

KEY STRENGTHS: Survival skills, leadership, CIA training, command of S.H.I.E.L.D. resources

APPEARANCES: IM2, CA:TFA, MTA, CA:TWS, A:AOU, A:IW, CM, A:E, TM

Heavy boots

DR. BRUCE BANNER

Hulk

Hulk is the alter ego of scientist Dr. Bruce Banner. Bruce's expertise with gamma radiation is useful to the Avengers, as is Hulk's overwhelming strength. At first Hulk's unrelenting power and anger prove too much for the team, and they fear awakening Bruce's other self. But, in time, Bruce unites both aspects of himself. He plays a key role in reversing the Blip.

Bruce's intellect and personality always in control

MAIN EVENT

On the planet Sakaar, Hulk ends up the reigning gladiator in a competition known as the Contest of Champions.

Flexible fabric doesn't tear

Legs able to jump hundreds of feet

MASTERING HIS POWERS

Tony Stark builds Bruce an isolated retreat in Mexico, where he learns to accept both of his identities through therapy and meditation. The new Bruce Banner-Hulk integration is deemed Smart Hulk.

Easily punches holes in brick walls

Time travel is uncharted territory for Bruce. Together again, the Avengers plan the ultimate heist to retrieve all six Infinity Stones and stop Thanos.

DATA FILE

AFFILIATION: Avengers, Contest of Champions, She-Hulk
KEY STRENGTHS: Scientific mind, creativity, resourcefulness; as Hulk: superhuman strength, durability, regeneration, distance jumping, speed, agility
APPEARANCES: TIH, MTA, A:AOU, T:R, A:IW, A:E, SH:AAL

THADDEUS ROSS

Secretary of State

Serving as Lieutenant General in the U.S. Army, Thaddeus Ross oversees a new Super Soldier Serum program. His daughter, Elizabeth, and Bruce Banner are recruited, but when Bruce transforms into the Hulk, Ross is intent on catching him. Ross is later appointed U.S. Secretary of State and tries to regulate the activities of the Avengers.

SOKOVIA ACCORDS
Ross enforces the Sokovia Accords: the government-controlled regulation of super-powered individuals. This brings him into conflict with the Avengers, who are not all in favor of the Accords.

Army uniform and medals swapped for suit

IN CHARGE
Ross is an authoritarian. He doesn't like being disobeyed. When Captain America and his partners refuse to sign the Sokovia Accords, Ross designates them as criminal fugitives.

In his desire to stop the Hulk, Ross plans to inject a sample of the Super Soldier Serum into Emil Blonsky, a soldier helping him track down Hulk.

DATA FILE
AFFILIATION: U.S. Army, U.S. State Department, Strategic Operations Command Center, Sokovia Accords
KEY STRENGTHS: Command of U.S. military and government resources
APPEARANCES: TIH, CA:CW, A:IW, A:E, BW

EMIL BLONSKY

Abomination

Soldier Emil Blonsky volunteered for a gamma radiation transformation to fight the Hulk. He became the monstrous Abomination, and caused massive damage. While in prison, Blonsky turns over a new leaf and finds inner peace. His best chance for parole? Lawyer and She-Hulk hero Jennifer Walters.

Attentive listener

Has control of massive strength

Loose clothing

GAMMA GURU

Following his release, Blonsky provides life coaching and spiritual consultation for others at his retreat. While he gives Jen a supportive space to talk about her feelings, he also offers wellness seminars as Abomination. They aren't cheap!

IN THE RING

Wong breaks Abomination out of prison to take part in an explosive fighting match at the Golden Daggers Club. It's all part of Wong's training to become the Sorcerer Supreme. After losing the face-off, Abomination returns to his cell quite calmly.

DATA FILE

AFFILIATION: Hulk, She-Hulk, Wong
KEY STRENGTHS: Superhuman strength, durability, speed, and agility, military training, charisma
APPEARANCES: TIH, SCATLOTTR, SH:AAL

Takes off shoes before transforming

Meditation has helped Blonsky stay in control when he's Abomination. He has no hard feelings for Wong at all.

NATASHA ROMANOFF
Black Widow

Natasha Romanoff was once a top Soviet assassin. S.H.I.E.L.D. agent Clint Barton was ordered to eliminate her, but he saw her potential and recruited her instead. She uses her spy skills for S.H.I.E.L.D., infiltrating Stark Industries, teaming up with Captain America, and battling alongside the other Avengers.

Black Widow tactical suit

Black Widow always adapts to changing situations. After the Blip, she leads the remaining Avengers team and makes the ultimate sacrifice to ensure their mission does not fail.

WIDOW'S BITE

Black Widow wears an electroshock "Widow's Bite" gauntlet on each wrist. They can incapacitate opponents on contact, or fire stun projectiles.

FOUND FAMILY

As a child, Natasha spent years undercover with fellow agents Alexei, Melina, and Yelena. She loves them as her own parents and sister before they separate. In time, she also considers her fellow Avengers her family.

Widow's Bite

Energy baton with retractable blade

Natasha has a long friendship with Tony Stark, from undercover assistant to the Sokovia Accords.

DATA FILE

AFFILIATION: S.H.I.E.L.D., Red Room, Avengers, Tony Stark, Captain America

KEY STRENGTHS: Red Room assassin training, martial arts, agility, spy skills, Widow's Bite gauntlets, electroshock batons

APPEARANCES: IM2, MTA, CA:TWS, A:AOU, CA:CW, A:IW, A:E, BW

JUSTIN HAMMER
Corporate rival

Hammer Industries is run by Justin Hammer, one of Tony Stark's biggest competitors. The inept CEO isn't capable of innovating anything successful himself. Instead, he steals corporate secrets from his rivals. Hammer tries to force engineer Ivan Vanko to duplicate Tony's Iron Man technology, but, as always, his plan fails.

Neatly groomed hair

Flashy patterned tie

Single-breasted three-piece suit with notched lapel

UPSET PLAN

Hammer's plan to steal Tony's tech backfires disastrously. Instead of building suits of armor like Hammer asks, Vanko builds robotic drones—all under his own control. Then he turns against Hammer, leaving him to face the legal consequences.

Hammer is in Monaco for a TV interview. But when the interviewer chooses to follow a story about Tony Stark instead, Hammer is furious.

DEFECTIVE HARDWARE

Hammer boasts a success over his rival when he takes over Tony's military contracts. However, nothing that Hammer installs actually functions correctly in battle.

DATA FILE

AFFILIATION: Hammer Industries, Seagate Prison, Ivan Vanko
KEY STRENGTHS: Manipulation, thievery, ambition
APPEARANCES: IM2

IVAN VANKO

Vengeful engineer

Ivan Vanko's father, Anton, helped Howard Stark invent the first Arc Reactor. But when Anton tried to sell the technology out from under Howard, he was deported, ending up in a Russian prison and living the rest of his life destitute. Ivan uses the technology to create a suit and seek revenge on Howard's son, Tony Stark.

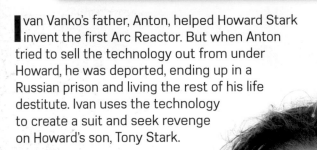

Unkempt hair

DATA FILE

AFFILIATION: Hammer Industries, Anton Vanko
KEY STRENGTHS:
Engineering genius; with suit: electro-whips, strength, flight
APPEARANCES: IM2

BIRTH OF A MENACE
After his father's death, Ivan builds a Repulsor Tech-powered suit of his own. The first suit is crude but powerful enough to challenge Iron Man.

WHIPPED INTO SHAPE
Ivan's RT (Repulsor Tech) channels energy to a pair of handheld electro-whips that are connected to his suit. They are strong enough to cut through most metals and even deflect Iron Man's powerful energy blasts.

External miniature RT (Ivan version)

Ivan bides his time, waiting for vengeance. He hacks into War Machine's suit, using it to attack Tony.

THOR
God of Thunder

Thor is the eldest son of Odin and Frigga, the king and queen of the realm of Asgard. After a brief exile on Earth, Thor joins the Avengers. Upon the passing of his father, Thor becomes king, although his world is destroyed by Ragnarok. After Thanos's defeat, Thor relinquishes his throne to Valkyrie and goes on new adventures. He finds the fulfillment he is looking for when he adopts the villain Gorr's daughter.

Signature red cape

Asgardian-style bracer

Thor can wield lightning without his hammers, but they focus the lightning's power.

Haft formed from Groot's arm

MIGHTY MJOLNIR

Thor's enchanted hammer, Mjolnir, was forged in the heart of a dying star. It can be wielded only by someone who is deemed worthy. When Mjolnir is destroyed by Hela, Thor asks Eitri the weapons forger to create a new axe called Stormbreaker.

Axe made at Nidavellir from power of neutron star

FIGHTING FOR EARTH

At the Battle of New York, Thor joins forces with Captain America and the Avengers to stop his brother Loki and the alien Chitauri invasion.

Leather boots

DATA FILE

AFFILIATION: Asgard, Avengers, Loki, Dr. Jane Foster, Korg, Guardians of the Galaxy

KEY STRENGTHS: Strength, agility, near-invulnerability, can summon lightning, power of Mjolnir and Stormbreaker

APPEARANCES: T, MTA, T:TDW, A:AOU, T:R, A:IW, A:E, T:LAT

LOKI

God of Mischief

TRICKSTER

Loki learns Asgardian magic from his mother, Frigga. His favorite magic tricks—mostly used for personal gain—include creating doppelgängers (identical copies of himself), changing his or others' appearance, and moving objects with his mind.

Loki is the adopted son of King Odin and Queen Frigga of Asgard. His biological father, King Laufey of the Frost Giants, abandoned him as a baby. Loki is jealous of his older brother, Thor. Although he rebels against his family, Loki later helps Thor save their people from the dangerous Hela. While he's adept at Asgardian magic, Loki's tricks are ultimately not enough to save him from Thanos.

Hair tangled from battle

Subtle tints of green, Loki's signature color

Protective pauldrons

DATA FILE

AFFILIATION: Asgard, Thor, Thanos, Chitauri invaders, Grandmaster
KEY STRENGTHS: Illusion magic, long life, rapid regeneration, deception
APPEARANCES: T, MTA, T:TDW, T:R, A:IW, A:E

During the Battle of New York, Loki wields the Mind Stone in his scepter, allowing him to control minds. It is one of six Infinity Stones. However, the Avengers thwart Loki's plans to rule over Earth.

BROTHERS IN ARMS

Thor releases Loki from prison to join forces against the Dark Elf Malekith. They grow closer over their adventures, but Loki would never admit it.

DR. JANE FOSTER

Leading astrophysicist

FLEETING LOVE

Thor and Jane Foster's romance is made difficult by Thor's long absences. Facing danger on a regular basis is also a lot for anyone to handle. As a result, Jane ends their relationship after a violent battle in Sokovia.

Brilliant scientist Dr. Jane Foster is one of the world's foremost astrophysicists and astronomers. She encounters Thor when he is banished to Earth, and the two quickly fall in love. Jane helps Thor to both redeem himself and save the universe from the Dark Elf Malekith and his apocalyptic weapon, the Aether.

Notebook on Bifrost phenomenon

WORTHY WARRIOR

While battling cancer, Jane hears the call of Mjolnir. The broken hammer reassembles itself and transforms her into The Mighty Thor. Jane uses the legendary weapon to save Asgard's children—and the universe. It's her final brave act.

Jane is one of the first to believe Thor when he appears on Earth. She drives him to find his hammer.

Winter jacket

Jane is angry with Loki for his misdeeds when she finally meets him on Asgard, though he later ends up saving her life when they confront Malekith.

Winter-proof hiking boots

DATA FILE

AFFILIATION: Thor, Dr. Erik Selvig, Culver University, Dr. Darcy Lewis
KEY STRENGTHS: Scientific mind, bravery, determination; as The Mighty Thor: control lighting, enhanced strength, speed, and durability, Mjolnir
APPEARANCES: T, T:TDW, T:LAT

ODIN

King of Asgard

Patch over eye lost in battle

Odin is the wise and powerful all-father, ruler of Asgard. His wife is Frigga, and his children are Hela, Thor, and Loki. Odin is known for being stern, but there is always a good reason for his strong-willed decrees. Though he is tough on his sons, and Loki rebels against him, Odin loves them both.

Golden disks

Odin sits on his throne wielding his spear. He uses it to harness incredible power as he rules over Asgard.

Folded hands convey confidence and quiet authority

Gold woven into tunic fabric

ASGARD SACKED
Odin surveys the damage after Asgard is ransacked by the Dark Elves. Grieving the loss of his wife, Odin locks down his kingdom.

Ceremonial royal Asgardian cape

FINAL REST
After he is stranded on Earth by Loki, Odin spends his last days in Norway with the aid of the sorcerer Doctor Strange. Upon bidding farewell to his sons, Odin joins his wife, Frigga, in Valhalla, the Asgardian afterlife.

DATA FILE
AFFILIATION: Asgard
KEY STRENGTHS: Leadership, strength, long life, spear
APPEARANCES: T, T:TDW, T:R

FRIGGA

Queen of Asgard

Thor and Loki's loving mother, Frigga, is devoted to her family. She speaks up for Thor during his exile. When Loki tries to seize the throne and ends up in prison, she pleads his case to her husband, Odin. Though Odin refuses to release Loki, Frigga trusts he has a plan. Frigga even encourages Thor when he visits from the future.

Glistening gemstones

A proud mother, Frigga stands beside Loki during Thor's coronation ceremony, before it is interrupted by thieving Frost Giants.

Traditional Asgardian knot patterns

FAMILY PROTECTOR
Frigga is a highly skilled sword fighter. She faces Malekith, leader of the Dark Elves, when he invades the palace. Frigga sacrifices herself to protect Dr. Jane Foster.

Royal gown for Thor's coronation

Green represents new beginnings

MAGICAL MOTHER
Frigga is a sorceress. She teaches magic to her younger son Loki to give him a competitive edge in battle.

DATA FILE
AFFILIATION: Asgard
KEY STRENGTHS: Magic, selfless love, sword fighting
APPEARANCES: T, T:TDW, A:E

LADY SIF

Asgardian powerhouse

Lady Sif is one of Asgard's greatest warriors and a close friend of Thor and the Warriors Three. She aids Thor during his exile and helps him escape from Asgard to fight the Dark Elves. Later, Lady Sif hunts Gorr the God Butcher, who is on a mission to destroy the gods in every realm. She loses her arm in their fight. After she recovers, she finds a new purpose: training New Asgard's children.

Toughened Asgardian steel

MYSTICAL BLADE

Sif's magical sword can extend into a double-bladed spear. The sword locks together with her shield and can be carried on her back. The sword is reforged after it is badly damaged while fighting the Destroyer.

Sword hilt

Shirt of chain mail beneath armor

Overlapping armor plates provide flexible protection

Bracer holds wrist wrap in place

Leather and chain mail skirt

MOUNTED COMBAT

Sif rides to war against pirate hordes on her mighty steed. A much-honored fighter, her horse is kept for her in the royal stables on Vanaheim.

Sif has feelings for Thor, but she hides them in case they spoil their friendship.

Lady Sif fights invading Marauders alongside Thor and the army of Asgard after the Bifrost is destroyed.

DATA FILE

AFFILIATION: Asgard, Thor, Warriors Three
KEY STRENGTHS: Strength, speed, agility, hand-to-hand combat
APPEARANCES: T, T:TDW, T:LAT

HEIMDALL
Gateway guardian

Heimdall is stationed at an observatory on the edge of Asgard's famed Bifrost, Asgard's gateway to the Nine Realms. Heimdall is tasked with guarding the Bifrost. He has the ability to see into the far reaches of the universe and allow others, such as Thor, to see through his eyes, too.

Horn-shaped helm

LOYALTY AND HONOR

Heimdall shows steadfast allegiance to Asgard's throne, and he defends his people to the death. He isn't afraid to break the rules, though, if there is a good enough reason.

MAGIC SWORD

Heimdall uses his sword to lock or unlock the Bifrost from his observatory. (Odin's spear can open the Bifrost as well.) In special circumstances, the sword can be used to activate the gateway from anywhere.

Heavy gleaming armor

Bronze bracers on forearm

Mighty sword activates Bifrost

Soft leather leggings

DATA FILE

AFFILIATION: Asgard
KEY STRENGTHS: Strength, sword fighting, long life, infinite sight, Bifrost control
APPEARANCES: T, T:TDW, T:R, A:IW

Heimdall is defeated by Thanos. In his final moments, Heimdall sends Hulk to Earth via the Bifrost to warn the Avengers that Thanos is coming. The Asgardian's quick thinking gives Earth's protectors time to prepare.

VOLSTAGG

Valiant warrior

Volstagg is a friend of Thor and, alongside comrades Fandral and Hogun, is one of the fabled Warriors Three. Lady Sif is the fifth member of their close-knit circle. A loyal companion, Volstagg readily comes to Thor's aid when he is exiled and helps battle the Destroyer. Volstagg is finally defeated by the vengeful Hela.

Long hair is typical of Asgardian warriors

VOLSTAGG THE VICTORIOUS

Volstagg is one of Asgard's greatest warriors. There are legendary tales of his battles across the Nine Realms.

Battle-worn pauldron

Hauberk (chain mail shirt)

READY AND ABLE

Volstagg has a big heart but poor judgment. He readily joins Thor and his friends on many misadventures, including an invasion of Jotunheim.

Forearm armor

Separate bracer for greater range of motion

Volstagg has a huge appetite. In truth, he savors victory banquets as much as the actual victory.

Etched steel battle axe

DATA FILE

AFFILIATION: Asgard, Thor, Lady Sif, Warriors Three
KEY STRENGTHS: Strength, stamina, loyalty
APPEARANCES: T, T:TDW, T:R

KING LAUFEY

King of the Frost Giants

King Laufey led his army of Frost Giants in
an invasion of Tønsberg, Norway, in 965 CE.
Odin and the forces of Asgard engaged them in
battle, forcing them back to their homeworld
on Jotunheim and defeating them there.
Laufey signed a peace treaty and gave
Odin his weapon of mass destruction,
the powerful Casket of Ancient Winters.

Laufey and the Frost Giants hide
among the icy ruins of Jotunheim,
where they look like part of the
bleak landscape.

Glowing red eyes

DATA FILE

AFFILIATION: Jotunheim, Frost
Giants, Loki
KEY STRENGTHS: Can form ice at
will or freeze anything on contact
APPEARANCES: T

THE END OF PEACE

When Thor and his friends invade
Jotunheim, Odin intervenes to
restore the peace treaty between
himself and Laufey. It is too late,
however: Laufey promises war.

Skin is ice-cold
to the touch

LOKI'S REVENGE

Laufey is Loki's biological
father, who abandoned
his son for being too
small. Loki was raised
instead by Odin. Years
later, Loki tricks Laufey
into invading Asgard.
He then eliminates
Laufey to save his
adoptive father, Odin.

DR. ERIK SELVIG

Scientific mentor

Theoretical physicist Dr. Erik Selvig is a mentor of Dr. Jane Foster and a friend of Thor's. He is hired by S.H.I.E.L.D. to study the Tesseract, a mysterious relic, but Thor's rebellious brother Loki takes control of Selvig's mind, temporarily frazzling his personality. Erik later supports Jane through her chemotherapy.

NEW RESEARCH
Erik and intern Darcy Lewis work with Jane in their rented office space in New Mexico. Their chance encounter with Thor leads them to debate all things Asgardian.

CLUED IN
Erik's theoretical work on the existence of other worlds makes him the perfect ally for Thor when the Asgardian finds himself on Earth.

Erik works on the top-secret Project Pegasus, studying the Tesseract. His aim is to unlock the power of this mystical object.

Loki's mind control took its toll on Erik. Darcy Lewis collects him from a police station after he is caught running around naked.

Tweed jacket

Bag contains scientific equipment

DATA FILE
AFFILIATION: Thor, Dr. Jane Foster, Dr. Darcy Lewis, Loki, S.H.I.E.L.D., Avengers
KEY STRENGTHS: Genius, expert knowledge of Asgardian mythology
APPEARANCES: T, MTA, T:TDW, A:AOU, T:LAT

DR. DARCY LEWIS
Witty scientist

Jane Foster and Erik Selvig are lucky to have an intern as smart and devoted as Darcy Lewis. She stays with them during the chaos of Thor's banishment on Earth. She manages to free Erik from a police station and, with the aid of her own intern, Ian Boothby, helps defeat the Dark Elves during their invasion.

LIVE AUDIENCE
Darcy becomes a doctor of astrophysics and works with S.W.O.R.D. The agency brings her in to figure out what's happening in the town of Westview, New Jersey. Darcy discovers a television signal coming from the town and gets sucked into Wanda Maximoff and Vision's new sitcom life—literally.

Burgundy beanie hat

Cozy scarf

Phone keeps Darcy in the know

At S.W.O.R.D.'s base outside Westview, Darcy tries to contact Wanda over the radio to find out more about the mysterious television show.

Gray wool toggle jacket

PILLAR OF THE TEAM
Darcy works tirelessly for Jane Foster and Erik Selvig, and later considers them close friends. She supports Jane during her illness.

DATA FILE
AFFILIATION: Thor, Dr. Jane Foster, Dr. Erik Selvig, S.W.O.R.D., Jimmy Woo, Captain Monica Rambeau
KEY STRENGTHS: Ingenuity, taking initiative, thinking outside the box
APPEARANCES: T, T:TDW, WV, T:LAT

IAN BOOTHBY

The intern

BUDDING SCIENTIST

Ian has a strong scientific background. He has an interest in ornithology and studies astronomy and physics in grad school. He hopes to follow in Dr. Foster's footsteps and become a leading scientist.

Simple winter cap

Dr. Foster's phase meter

Casual cargo pants

DATA FILE

AFFILIATION: Dr. Darcy Lewis, Dr. Erik Selvig, Dr. Jane Foster
KEY STRENGTHS: Helpful, enthusiastic, loyal
APPEARANCES: T:TDW

Hiking boots

Ian Boothby is an unpaid intern who assists Darcy Lewis, the intern of Dr. Jane Foster. The London university student is working for Darcy when they discover a strange network of inter-dimensional portals leading to Svartalfheim, homeworld of the vengeful Dark Elves. Ian helps Darcy find Dr. Erik Selvig when Jane leaves, and then does all he can to help thwart the Dark Elves.

RUNNING OUT OF TIME

Ian and Darcy hammer gravimetric spikes into the ground in Greenwich, England. They watch as the leader of the Dark Elves, Malekith, arrives and battles Thor.

Ian is a quiet yet helpful intern, willing to help where he can. He poses as Erik's son to free him from custody and later saves Darcy's life.

DESTROYER

Vault guardian

The warden of Odin's vault is known as the Destroyer. The robotlike sentry has no mechanical parts. It is a magical armored soldier charged with protecting Odin's most valuable weapons and dealing retribution upon the all-father's enemies. When the Destroyer attacks Thor on Earth, it is vanquished with the power of the Thunder God's hammer, Mjolnir.

"Eyes" open to emit deadly blasts

CONTROLLED REMOTELY

The Destroyer is controlled by the spear of the king of Asgard. The Destroyer will obey anyone who wields the spear, including Loki when he takes the throne.

Magically transforming metallic body

Virtually indestructible armor

DATA FILE

AFFILIATION: Asgard, Odin, Loki
KEY STRENGTHS: Strength, near invincibility, energy blasts
APPEARANCES: T

DESTROYER UNLEASHED

The Destroyer arrives on Earth under the control of Loki, with a mission to eliminate Thor. Lady Sif and the Warriors Three try to stop him, without success.

Heavy metal feet can crush enemies

Thor hopes his brother, Loki, will be merciful but submits himself to the Destroyer to save the town.

JASPER SITWELL

Hydra double agent

Jasper Sitwell is a long-serving S.H.I.E.L.D. agent with a wealth of experience. Agent Phil Coulson assigns Sitwell to cover up the New Mexico incident involving Thor and his hammer. Sitwell is also charged with locating Loki prior to the Chitauri invasion. However, Sitwell is later proven to be a secret Hydra agent.

DATA FILE

AFFILIATION: S.H.I.E.L.D., Hydra
KEY STRENGTHS: Hydra and S.H.I.E.L.D. training, high security clearance
APPEARANCES: T, MTA, CA:TWS, A:E

Smart and devious mind

S.H.I.E.L.D. lapel pin amuses other Hydra loyalists

TAKING THE LEAD

Sitwell takes over when Steve Rogers disobeys orders from his superiors. Sitwell orders Brock Rumlow and his S.T.R.I.K.E. team to hunt Steve down.

Sitwell is an office worker. He orders others into danger while he remains safe.

UNDERVALUED

Like most Hydra agents, Sitwell thinks he is a good guy. Nonetheless, his boss, Alexander Pierce, believes he is a liability to their cause and sends the Winter Soldier to eliminate him.

STEVE ROGERS

Captain America

Vibranium shield designed by industrialist Howard Stark

Avengers "A" logo on shoulder

The Super Soldier Serum transforms Steve Rogers into the Super Hero Captain America (aka Cap). After defeating the Red Skull, Cap spends years frozen in a block of ice. He wakes in the present day and takes charge of the Avengers. Cap leads them against aliens, robots, terrorists, and even keeps them from destroying one another. His strength as a leader brings the divided team of heroes back together to fight Thanos. After their victory, he reunites with the love of his life.

BATTLE DRESS
Captain America's suit (designed with help from S.H.I.E.L.D. agent Phil Coulson) evolves over time, becoming less showy. The patriotic design endures until Cap joins the battle to save the world from the warlord Thanos and his alien army.

WORTHY LEADER
Captain America stands alongside Iron Man and Thor when Thanos attacks the Avengers Compound. Cap picks up Thor's hammer and knocks back Thanos with a mighty swing.

DATA FILE
AFFILIATION: U.S. Army, S.S.R. (Strategic Scientific Reserve), Howling Commandos, Avengers, S.H.I.E.L.D., Peggy Carter
KEY STRENGTHS: Strength, agility, speed, endurance, leadership, support
APPEARANCES: CA:TFA, MTA, CA:TWS, A:AOU, CA:CW, A:IW, A:E

Armored gaiters protect lower legs

Cap refuses to give up. Whether it's the war on Hydra or a battle with the entire universe at stake, he keeps fighting.

JAMES "BUCKY" BARNES
Winter Soldier

James "Bucky" Barnes is a childhood friend of Steve Rogers. The friends reunite during World War II, but Bucky is captured by Hydra and experimented on by Dr. Arnim Zola. His brain is reprogrammed to transform him into a super soldier secret weapon, known as the Winter Soldier. In time, and with the support of Steve, he overcomes Hydra's indoctrination and remembers his life as Bucky.

Mind no longer influenced by Winter Soldier activation code

Secret kill switch detaches arm

DATA FILE
AFFILIATION: Hydra, Avengers, Captain America, Falcon
KEY STRENGTHS: Strength, speed, agility, endurance, cybernetic arm
APPEARANCES: CA:TFA, CA:TWS, CA:CW, A:IW, A:E, TFATWS

Vibranium prosthetic hand and arm created by Wakandan scientists

ACT OF WAR
Helmut Zemo frames Bucky for the Sokovia Accords bombing, placing Bucky at the heart of the Avengers' civil war. After learning the truth, T'Challa gives Bucky refuge and recovery in Wakanda.

Physical abilities enhanced by Hydra experiments

ATONEMENT
When his programming is active, the Winter Soldier is a remorseless assassin. After the Blip, Bucky receives a pardon but keeps a list of amends to make to the people he wronged while he was brainwashed.

Bucky and Rocket make a good team during the battle in Wakanda. Rocket envies Bucky's high-powered weapon, though.

Tactical boot gaiters

JOHANN SCHMIDT
The Red Skull

The appearance of Nazi officer Johann Schmidt is dramatically altered when he is injected with an early version of the Super Soldier Serum. The formula also boosts Schmidt's physical performance and heartless ambition. He takes the code name "the Red Skull." This cunning mastermind—and head of the Nazi science division known as Hydra—next sets his sights on a powerful relic called the Tesseract.

Face transformed by serum

Impatient with Dr. Arnim Zola's cautious approach, Schmidt unleashes the full power of the Tesseract.

DATA FILE

AFFILIATION: Hydra, Soul Stone
KEY STRENGTHS: Intelligence, ambition, Tesseract energy weapons, Hydra's resources, Super Soldier Serum; on Vormir: wraithlike existence, levitation
APPEARANCES: CA:TFA, A:IW, A:E

Silver belt buckle with Hydra emblem

BAD TO WORSE
The Super Soldier Serum amplifies characteristics already present in the recipient. For the Red Skull, this includes a strong ego, determination, and a dangerous thirst for power.

Leather trench coat

DRIVING INTO BATTLE
The Red Skull's custom armored car is the envy of his colleagues. The engine is powered by Tesseract energy, managed by a dashboard lined with extra gauges.

Military boots

The Tesseract banishes the Red Skull to the planet Vormir, where he guides those who seek the Soul Stone.

PEGGY CARTER

Steadfast spy

Agent Peggy Carter serves in the British Air Force and Special Air Service before joining the Strategic Scientific Reserve (S.S.R.) in 1940. Peggy oversees the training of Project Rebirth candidates at Camp Lehigh, where she meets Steve Rogers. The two fall in love but are tragically separated for nearly 70 years. In one special timeline, Steve and Peggy do get their happily ever after.

DATA FILE

AFFILIATION: U.S. military, S.S.R., Project Rebirth, S.H.I.E.L.D., Captain America
KEY STRENGTHS: Determination, wisdom, loyalty, self-sacrifice
APPEARANCES: CA:TFA, CA:TWS, A:AOU, AM, CA:CW, A:E

Metal S.S.R. insignia

FEARLESS AGENT

Agent Carter doesn't wait around for orders. She chases assassin Heinz Kruger on foot after he infiltrates the S.S.R. lab.

Peggy is Steve Rogers's biggest supporter. She accompanies him to the lab where he is transformed.

Two-piece wool dress uniform

Peggy remains a top S.H.I.E.L.D. commander for years. She oversees Hank Pym and Janet Van Dyne's missions.

S.H.I.E.L.D. FOUNDER

Peggy Carter's contributions are undervalued by S.S.R. management until Howard Stark asks her to help him create a secret organization known as S.H.I.E.L.D.

TIMOTHY "DUM DUM" DUGAN

Howling Commando leader

Sergeant Timothy Dugan is a founding member of the Howling Commandos team. They are led by Captain America, and their objective is to defeat the secret Nazi research organization Hydra. Dugan takes command of the team following Cap's disappearance. After the war, Dum Dum works with S.H.I.E.L.D. on missions to keep America safe.

Dum Dum's signature bowler hat

Thick handlebar mustache

FIGHT FOR JUSTICE
Dum Dum is a close friend of Bucky Barnes. They are both taken prisoner by Hydra during World War II and later rescued by Captain America. Their experience in captivity motivates them to join forces and wipe out Hydra.

BIRTH OF THE HOWLERS
After their rescue from Hydra, Dum Dum and his comrades recuperate in London. There, Captain America asks them to join his team. Dum Dum agrees but insists that Cap first buys them a round of drinks.

Wool army pants

DATA FILE
AFFILIATION: U.S. Army, S.S.R., S.H.I.E.L.D., Captain America, Howling Commandos
KEY STRENGTHS: Commitment, honor, bravery, U.S. Army training
APPEARANCES: CA:TFA

Dum Dum leads the Howling Commandos in their capture of the Red Skull's Hydra headquarters in the Swiss Alps.

GABE JONES

Weapons expert

U.S. Infantry garrison cap

U.S. Army uniform

After graduating from university, Gabe Jones joined the U.S. Army's 92nd Infantry, a division of Black soldiers. He is later captured and forced to build weapons for Hydra. Jones is freed when Captain America arrives to rescue another captive, Bucky Barnes. Jones subsequently joins the Howling Commandos as their heavy weapons specialist.

STRONGER TOGETHER

Gabe Jones and Dum Dum Dugan are good friends, having served in the army together. They escape from a Hydra prison camp aboard a stolen tank.

IN THE FIELD

Gabe is a handy teammate to have behind enemy lines. He serves as the Howlers' interpreter and is also good at adapting any unusual Hydra weapons and vehicles that they manage to capture.

DATA FILE

AFFILIATION: U.S. Army, Howling Commandos
KEY STRENGTHS: Speaks German and French, army training, marksmanship
APPEARANCES: CA:TFA

JACQUES DERNIER

Demolitions specialist

Jacques Dernier is from Marseille, France. During World War II, he was captured by the Nazis and sent to a Hydra labor camp and weapons factory. There he befriended Dum Dum Dugan and his other future Howling Commandos teammates. After their escape, he became the Howlers' explosives expert.

BOMBER

Jacques Dernier hones his bomb-making skills by sabotaging Hydra equipment while a prisoner. His antics cost him a week without food rations. He delights in blowing up Hydra tanks when he is eventually freed.

French wool cap

SELF-MADE SOLDIER

Jacques Dernier was an operative in the French Resistance. He is the only Howling Commando who was not officially a soldier in an Allied army.

Wrinkled shirt

DATA FILE

AFFILIATION: French Resistance, Howling Commandos, Captain America
KEY STRENGTHS: Explosives expert
APPEARANCES: CA:TFA

JAMES MONTGOMERY FALSWORTH

Talented tactician

British paratrooper beret with Union Flag badge

Mills Bomb (hand grenade)

MANY MEDALS

Falsworth is the most decorated Howler. His service medals include the Order of Burma, Africa Star, War Medal, and Defense Medal.

James Montgomery Falsworth is an expert battle strategist. He hails from Birmingham, England, and served as a Major in His Majesty's 3rd Independent Parachute Regiment. Falsworth was taken prisoner by Hydra in 1943 and forced to work in a weapons factory before escaping and joining the Howling Commandos.

Ammo belt

Pouch with three ammo clips

Wool and leather jacket

Following their escape from Hydra, Falsworth and friends are asked by Steve Rogers to join the Howling Commandos. Falsworth enlists first.

DATA FILE

AFFILIATION: Howling Commandos, Captain America
KEY STRENGTHS: Tactical mind, paratrooper training, espionage, marksmanship
APPEARANCES: CA:TFA

WAR ON HYDRA

As a member of the Howling Commandos, Falsworth helps plan a campaign to eliminate Hydra from Europe.

Cotton gaiters over leather boots

JIM MORITA

Oustanding operator

Jim Morita is a Japanese American from Fresno, California. He served in the U.S. Army until he was captured by Hydra and forced to work in an enemy weapons factory. After escaping, he joins the Howling Commandos as their communications specialist, intercepting secret transmissions.

U.S. Army knitted wool jeep cap

RADIO MAN

As a communications expert, Morita intercepts Hydra's coded messages, allowing him to locate Hydra scientist Arnim Zola aboard a train. Morita also facilitates Steve Rogers's last call to Peggy Carter before Steve crashes in Antarctica.

U.S. Army jacket

THE LONG HAUL

Morita and the Howlers' campaign to rid Europe of Hydra continues through a cold winter in the Alps until they capture the Red Skull's secret base.

DATA FILE

AFFILIATION: Howling Commandos, Captain America, U.S. Army
KEY STRENGTHS: Radio and telecommunications expertise, tech enthusiast, marksmanship
APPEARANCES: CA:TFA

DR. ARNIM ZOLA

Engineering genius

Hydra's top scientist is Dr. Arnim Zola, the second-in-command to Johann Schmidt (aka the Red Skull). Zola develops high-tech weapons and other advanced technology for Hydra. Zola wasn't always a fanatic, but his devotion grew under the leadership of the Red Skull. Nonetheless, Zola betrays his commander to save himself.

Fedora from stylish Berlin boutique

Zola is recruited as a scientist by S.H.I.E.L.D. after World War II. However, he uses his position to rebuild Hydra in secret.

Bow tie has become a signature look

Hydra pin

SEEKER OF POWER
Zola harnesses the limitless energy of the Tesseract (itself powered by an Infinity Stone) to build weapons for Hydra.

THOUGHT CONTROL
Before dying, Zola's mind is transferred to a mainframe computer. In this state, he develops an algorithm used by Hydra to eliminate threats.

DATA FILE
AFFILIATION: Hydra, S.H.I.E.L.D.
KEY STRENGTHS: Scientific genius, strong survival instinct
APPEARANCES: CA:TFA, CA:TWS

HEINZ KRUGER

Hydra assassin

Heinz Kruger is a devoted Hydra agent sent to recover the Super Soldier Serum from the Strategic Scientific Reserve (S.S.R.) lab and eliminate the defector, Dr. Abraham Erskine. He infiltrates Project Rebirth using the identity of State Department agent Fred Clemson. Once caught, Kruger takes his life by ingesting a cyanide capsule.

Tense expression

Cyanide capsule hidden in tooth

Smart three-piece suit

MAN WITH A PLAN

Kruger detonates a bomb on the balcony of the S.S.R. lab, just before stealing the Super Soldier Serum, shooting Dr. Erskine, and fleeing to his car.

Kruger attempts to escape in the *Fieser Dorsch* mini submarine.

HARD TO STOP

As he flees the S.S.R. lab, Kruger is nearly shot by Agent Carter. The assassin continues, determined to make his escape, until Steve Rogers pulls him from his departing submarine.

DATA FILE

AFFILIATION: Hydra
KEY STRENGTHS: Hydra training, espionage, marksmanship
APPEARANCES: CA:TFA

DR. ABRAHAM ERSKINE

Super soldier creator

A talented German scientist, Dr. Abraham Erskine got Hitler's attention by developing a Super Soldier Serum. Nazi officer Johann Schmidt captures Erskine and forces the scientist to inject him with the untested formula. When Erskine escapes, he joins the U.S. Strategic Scientific Reserve (S.S.R.) and their Project Rebirth.

Felt fedora hat

Prescription glasses

DATA FILE

AFFILIATION: S.S.R., Project Rebirth
KEY STRENGTHS: Scientific mind, wisdom, kindness, moral character
APPEARANCES: CA:TFA

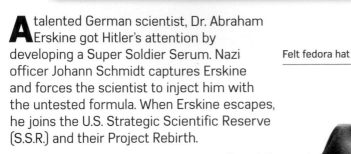

APPROVAL

Impressed with Steve Rogers's five attempts to enlist, Erskine approves his U.S. military application.

Concerned for Steve Rogers, Erskine tells Howard Stark to stop the experiment, but Steve wants to continue.

Custom three-piece suit

FINDING A HERO

Erskine's super soldier formula amplifies the personality of the recipient. Therefore, Erskine selects a good man to be the test subject: Steve Rogers.

HOWARD STARK

Inventor and businessman

MANY TALENTS

Howard Stark is an engineer, inventor, entrepreneur, risk-taker, and astute businessman. His confident personality rubs some people the wrong way, including his son, Tony, although Tony learns to appreciate his father later in life.

Slick haircut

Stylishly cut gray suit

Howard Stark is the father of Tony Stark. During World War II, he is a member of the Strategic Scientific Reserve (S.S.R.) and develops equipment for Captain America and his Howling Commandos. Following the war, Howard founds S.H.I.E.L.D. with Peggy Carter. He later angers Hank Pym by trying to duplicate Ant-Man technology.

REVERSE ENGINEERING

Hydra creates advanced technology by studying the mystical object known as the Tesseract. Howard examines captured Hydra hardware to make something even better for Allied forces.

Howard Stark builds and maintains all the technology in the S.S.R. labs. He takes charge of the controls during Steve Rogers's transformation.

There were other more complex designs to choose from, but Captain America chooses a round vibranium shield created by Howard Stark.

DATA FILE

AFFILIATION: S.S.R., S.H.I.E.L.D., Stark Industries
KEY STRENGTHS: Ambition, scientific genius, creativity, wealth
APPEARANCES: IM2, CA:TFA, AM, CA:CW, A:E

CLINT BARTON

Hawkeye

The S.H.I.E.L.D. agent Clint Barton (code name: Hawkeye) is an expert bowman armed with an arsenal of trick arrows. He becomes a founding member of the Avengers during an alien invasion. Clint tries to retire to be with his family but is drawn into the Avengers' civil war. During the Blip, he works as a lawless vigilante hunting criminals. Clint finds some emotional release when he helps his new protégé, Kate Bishop, after she gets caught up in the New York City criminal underworld.

Trick arrows include acid and Pym Particles

A LONG HISTORY

Clint and Natasha Romanoff have a close relationship. When Natasha was a Soviet agent, S.H.I.E.L.D. ordered Clint to eliminate her. However, seeing her potential, he recruited her instead. Clint is devastated when Natasha sacrifices herself to save him, the Avengers' mission, and the universe.

During the Battle of New York, Hawkeye perches near Stark Tower, hitting invading Chitauri chariots with explosive arrows.

Lightweight body armor

Bent knees help Hawkeye pull bowstring further

MASTER ARCHER

Hawkeye is a left-handed bowman. His custom bow features remote controls for a mechanized quiver, which prepares trick arrowheads. Hawkeye's arrowheads feature rappelling lines, EMPs, flash arrowheads, timed explosives, and impact triggers.

DATA FILE

AFFILIATION: Barton family, S.H.I.E.L.D., Avengers, Black Widow, Kate Bishop
KEY STRENGTHS: Expert bowman with trick arrows, S.H.I.E.L.D. training, acrobatic abilities
APPEARANCES: T, MTA, A:AOU, CA:CW, A:E, H

Waterproof boots

THANOS

Ruthless warlord

Powerful Titan warlord Thanos is intent on eliminating half of the universe's population. He believes this will create balance by stabilizing resources. Thanos raises an army and acquires the powerful Infinity Stones, granting him absolute power to realize his diabolical purpose. He is defeated only when the Avengers undertake a Time Heist and use the stones to undo his foul actions.

Thanos has impressive strength. He easily defeats and humiliates Hulk aboard Thor's captured ship.

Infinity Gauntlet with all six stones

Closed fist activates gauntlet

BETRAYAL

Thanos has a complex relationship with his adopted daughter Gamora, whom he kidnapped as a child. She tries to eliminate him on Knowhere before he acquires all the stones.

THE INFINITY GAUNTLET

Thanos forces the Dwarf Eitri to forge a gauntlet that can harness the power of the Infinity Stones. The six stones control space, time, power, minds, souls, and reality. One by one, the villainous Thanos takes them all.

Thanos acquires the last Infinity Stone from Vision's forehead. Wearing the gauntlet, Thanos snaps his fingers in a moment called the Snap and extinguishes half of the universe.

DATA FILE

AFFILIATION: Chitauri army, Ronan the Accuser
KEY STRENGTHS: Strength, stamina, Infinity Gauntlet, Chitauri army
APPEARANCES: GOTG, A:IW, A:E

MARIA HILL

S.H.I.E.L.D. Deputy Director

Stark Industries
encrypted earpiece

Agent Maria Hill is the Deputy Director of S.H.I.E.L.D. She works closely with Director Nick Fury. While they don't always agree, Hill's forthright feedback is intended to provide Fury with credible alternatives. When Hydra takes over S.H.I.E.L.D. and Fury is forced to fake his own death, Hill is the only person he completely trusts.

TACTICAL SPECIALIST

Like her boss, Hill works confidently from the command center of a S.H.I.E.L.D. Helicarrier. She provides vital support during the Battle of New York and the Ultron Offensive in Sokovia.

FURY'S RIGHT HAND

After the collapse of S.H.I.E.L.D., Hill works undercover for Fury. She becomes a secret channel of communication from him to the Avengers and other covert agents embedded in the field.

Fire-resistant
S.H.I.E.L.D.
jumpsuit

Hill continues to work with the Avengers as an employee of Stark Industries, providing mission critical support.

Sturdy
boots for
fieldwork

DATA FILE

AFFILIATION: S.H.I.E.L.D., Avengers, Stark Industries, Nick Fury
KEY STRENGTHS: Determination, leadership, S.H.I.E.L.D. training
APPEARANCES: MTA, CA:TWS, A:AOU, A:IW, CM, A:E

CHITAURI
Alien invaders

The Chitauri are cyborg aliens who serve in Thanos's army. He uses them to devastate planets like Gamora's homeworld. Thanos lends the Chitauri to Loki for his own conquest of Earth, but the invasion fails. As a result, the aliens' advanced weapons fall into the hands of human criminals and terrorists. The Chitauri later fight as part of Thanos's forces in the Battle of Earth.

DATA FILE

AFFILIATION: Thanos, Loki, The Other
KEY STRENGTHS: Strength, numbers, Leviathan ships, advanced alien weapons
APPEARANCES: MTA, A:IW, A:E

Metal-fused skull plate

A FATAL FLAW
The Chitauri are seemingly endless in number, but they have one major weakness. Their hive mind requires connection to a mother ship. The Chitauri are stranded and perish when the Avengers destroy their ship and close their wormhole.

MANHATTAN MAYHEM
Once they reach New York, Chitauri forces detach from their massive Leviathans and begin their assault on the city. Pilots on flying chariots battle the Avengers in the skies.

Breathing apparatus

Metallic exoskeleton

Energy cannon

Double thumbs

The Chitauri army first arrives on Earth through a wormhole opened by Dr. Selvig using a relic known as the Tesseract.

MATTHEW ELLIS

President of the United States

ENEMIES UNKNOWN

President Ellis previously banned the scientific research of Advanced Idea Mechanics (AIM), an organization run by the shadowy Aldrich Killian. Killian plans to take revenge against President Ellis by assassinating him and taking control of the White House.

Well-tended hair for cameras

Following a series of explosions that are blamed on a terrorist known as the Mandarin, President Matthew Ellis steps up. He rebrands military hero War Machine as the Iron Patriot and orders him to hunt down the Mandarin. President Ellis, however, is unaware that a former acquaintance of his, Aldrich Killian, is the true terrorist.

Finely tailored suit

BAD PUBLICITY

Killian's bodyguard, Eric Savin, kidnaps President Ellis by placing him inside the Iron Patriot armor and flying him back to Killian. Killian intends to assassinate President Ellis on TV.

Dual microphones

DATA FILE

AFFILIATION: U.S. government
KEY STRENGTHS: Authority of the Presidency
APPEARANCES: IM3

ALDRICH KILLIAN

Extreme enemy

Aldrich Killian met Tony Stark in 1999, hoping to discuss his research agency AIM, but Stark brushed him off. Years later, Killian teams up with scientist Maya Hansen to develop her Extremis treatment, using it on his own body. He covers up Extremis's explosive side effects by employing an actor who impersonates a villain named the Mandarin.

Well-groomed hair

Custom-tailored suit

DATA FILE

AFFILIATION: AIM, the Mandarin, Maya Hansen, Eric Savin
KEY STRENGTHS: Strength, rapid regeneration, generates extreme heat, breathing fire
APPEARANCES: IM3

Rings are valuable and unusual

Body has super-powers following Extremis treatment

Killian explains Extremis to Pepper Potts, hoping to gain Stark Industries' support for his experimental research.

HOT UNDER THE COLLAR

Extremis reprograms human DNA to heal the body rapidly, repairing injuries, curing disease, regrowing lost limbs, and improving overall physical performance. Adverse effects include uncontrollable heat radiation and explosions. Killian can even breathe fire.

LAST STAND

Aldrich Killian and Tony Stark fight aboard Killian's oil tanker, *Norco*. With Extremis active in his system, Killian is a formidable adversary.

Expensive, fancy shoes

MAYA HANSEN

Extremis inventor

Maya Hansen is the genetics genius who created Extremis, a treatment that rewrites DNA to heal injuries. Unfortunately, Extremis has a terrible side effect where most recipients rapidly heat up and sometimes explode. Hansen is trying to stabilize it in her work at Aldrich Killian's research agency, AIM.

DATA FILE
AFFILIATION: AIM, Aldrich Killian
KEY STRENGTHS: Scientific genius, deception
APPEARANCES: IM3

SECRET LAIR
Hansen conducts her experiments in a secret lab with 40 scientists and a handful of test subjects.

Warm sweater for working in cold basement lab

CONFLICTED
Maya Hansen is driven to create Extremis by the desire to help people. She partners with Killian for funding, even though she knows he is in it for the wrong reasons. Hansen eventually sides with Tony Stark, but by then it is too late.

Hansen gains Pepper Potts's confidence by pretending to betray Killian, but it's actually a ruse to kidnap Potts.

ERIC SAVIN

Enhanced bodyguard

DATA FILE

AFFILIATION: AIM, Aldrich Killian, the Mandarin
KEY STRENGTHS: Extreme heat generation, rapid regeneration, enhanced strength
APPEARANCES: IM3

Retired Lieutenant Colonel Eric Savin is injected by Aldrich Killian with the Extremis treatment to heal his war injuries. He works as Killian's bodyguard and suits up in Rhodey Rhodes's stolen Iron Patriot armor to board Air Force One and kidnap the President. Savin meets his end fighting an Iron Man drone.

Focused mind keeps Extremis in check

HOTHEAD

The Extremis treatment inside Savin allows him to heal instantly after an injury—he can even regrow a foot. Extremis also causes him to generate massive internal heat.

MULTITASKER

As Killian's right-hand man, Savin has many duties, including coordinating covert missions for the other Extremis candidates. He also leads a helicopter assault that completely destroys Tony Stark's Malibu mansion.

Body has elevated temperature

Savin crosses paths with Tony Stark's bodyguard, Happy Hogan.

TREVOR SLATTERY

The Mandarin

Trevor Slattery is a failed British actor. He is hired by criminal mastermind Aldrich Killian to pose as a terrorist known as the Mandarin, leader of The Ten Rings. Slattery creates videos taking credit for explosions that are actually caused by Killian's genetic treatment, Extremis. Slattery is caught and sent to prison, where he is kidnapped by the real leader of The Ten Rings, Wenwu.

Long hair in bun

A CHARACTER

The Mandarin uses sunglasses to appear mysterious, but in reality, Slattery is kind and gentle. After Shang-Chi and Xialing—Wenwu's children—liberate Slattery, he helps them find the village of Ta Lo.

Gaudy costume jewelry rings

TELEVISION MENACE

The Mandarin rambles on in his videos, not making a lot of sense, but it sounds terrifying. His real purpose isn't to convey a specific ideology. He doesn't even know what he's saying—or that the public thinks he is real!

The Mandarin uses a mixture of carved symbols and violence in his video backdrops.

DATA FILE

AFFILIATION: AIM, Seagate Prison, The Ten Rings (fake), Morris
KEY STRENGTHS: Acting, communicating with the mystical creature Morris
APPEARANCES: IM3, SCATLOTTR

IRON PATRIOT

Stars and stripes

Tony Stark creates a new armor suit and gives it to his friend Rhodey Rhodes to replace his War Machine Mark I armor. This new War Machine Mark II armor is then painted red, white, and blue and renamed Iron Patriot by the U.S. Air Force to sound less threatening.

Cannon sits on articulated arm

Retractable face plate

Weaponry concealed in wrists

UNPATRIOTIC PLOT
Iron Patriot is given the task of hunting down the terrorist known as the Mandarin, but he is lured into a trap by the sinister Aldrich Killian. Killian kidnaps Rhodey and steals his armor.

Killian's henchman, Eric Savin, wears the Iron Patriot armor and boards Air Force One to kidnap the President.

Stabilizer belt balances armor during flight

Palms fitted with repulsors

DISARMING
Rhodey's new armor is an improvement on his old armor. However, it has been modified by AIM, Aldrich Killian's research agency. The U.S. Air Force trusts Killian, unaware of his plan to kidnap the President.

Thruster boots controlled by A.I. system

DATA FILE
AFFILIATION: U.S. Air Force, Tony Stark
KEY STRENGTHS: Flight, strength, missiles, repulsor beams, sonic cannon
APPEARANCES: IM3

HARLEY KEENER

Young ally

Harley Keener lives with his mother in Rose Hill, Tennessee. One night, he encounters a distressed Tony Stark in his garage, trying to mend his broken Iron Man armor. Harley helps Tony and shows him around town. The boy gets caught up in a fight between Tony Stark and dangerous villain Eric Savin but breaks free with Tony's help.

DATA FILE

AFFILIATION: Tony Stark
KEY STRENGTHS: Resourceful, helpful, interest in science and engineering, potato gun building skills
APPEARANCES: IM3, A:E

Button-up shirt for school

BUDDING SCIENTIST
Though Tony departs without much of a goodbye, he appreciates Harley's help. Tony sends the boy a haul of robots, computers, science equipment, and a new potato gun.

Backpack full of books and potatoes

UNLIKELY FRIENDS
Harley helps Tony Stark find the site of an explosion where a local man, Chad Davis, died. He then takes Tony to meet Davis's mother at a local bar. Harley's support helps Tony uncover part of a dangerous conspiracy.

Harley is a temporary custodian of Tony's Iron Man Mark XLII armor while it recharges in his garage.

Sneakers nearly outgrown

MALEKITH

Dark Elf warlord

Malekith is the vengeful leader of the Dark Elves. He is so old that the present universe is toxic to him. Malekith waits in hibernation for 5,000 years until the Convergence, when the Nine Realms overlap. His plan is to release a weapon, the Aether, and spread darkness across the universe.

Striking silver armor

Malekith and his forces make their final stand in Greenwich, England, the focal point of the Convergence.

Gloves needed to touch toxic objects

MASTER OF PATIENCE

The Aether is an ancient force of infinite destruction that resembles a red cloud of fluid and gas. Odin's father, Bor, steals the Aether and hides it from Malekith, but the Dark Elf waits for eons until Dr. Jane Foster rediscovers it.

DATA FILE

AFFILIATION: Dark Elves, Aether, Infinity Stones
KEY STRENGTHS: Strength, durability, regeneration, long life, Dark Elf army, Aether
APPEARANCES: T:TDW

TOTAL CONTROL

Malekith draws the Aether out of Dr. Foster and infects himself. The Aether is an Infinity Stone that controls reality, but its incredible power comes at a deadly cost.

Boots prevent contact with the elements

SAM WILSON

Falcon / Captain America

After retiring from military service, former U.S. Air Force pararescue officer Sam Wilson finds work at Veterans Affairs. He befriends Steve Rogers and helps him and Natasha Romanoff combat Hydra under the code name Falcon. Sam joins the Avengers and fights against Thanos's invasion of Wakanda— and at the final battle against Thanos. When Steve decides to retire, he presents his Captain America shield to Sam.

Thermal imaging goggles

DATA FILE

AFFILIATION: U.S. Air Force, Avengers, Steve Rogers, Bucky Barnes, Joaquin Torres, Sarah Wilson

KEY STRENGTHS: Air Force training; as Falcon: flight, shields (via wings), Redwing drone; as Captain America: vibranium shield

APPEARANCES: CA:TWS, A:AOU, AM, CA:CW, A:IW, A:E, TFATWS

Symbol of Captain America

FLIGHT AND FIGHT

Falcon's exosuit is fitted with integrated miniature jet engines, which power his flight. The wings can be used as weapons.

Vibranium shield passed down by Steve Rogers

Sam's Redwing drone launches on voice command and features retractable wings, twin machine guns, and remote scanning cameras.

Gauntlets protect from elements as well as impact

Flexible wings for flight and defense

Armored boots

CAPTAIN AMERICA

After talking with his sister, Sarah, Sam decides to take the mantle of Captain America. Wakandan engineers build his new high-tech, winged suit. It's equipped to carry multiple Redwing drones on the back.

SHARON CARTER

Code name: Agent 13

STRONG-WILLED

Sharon has a habit of going against her superiors—both at S.H.I.E.L.D. and the CIA. She chooses the side she thinks is right. This isolates her and creates enemies. After years as a fugitive, Sharon takes a more mercenary approach to life.

Hood up to keep low profile

Inspired to follow in the footsteps of her great-aunt Peggy Carter, Sharon Carter joins S.H.I.E.L.D. Nick Fury assigns her to watch over Steve Rogers. After the fall of S.H.I.E.L.D., Sharon gets a job with the CIA and Everett Ross. But when she helps Steve Rogers protect Bucky Barnes, she's deemed an enemy of the state and goes on the run.

Expensive leather coat

Pocket holds untraceable phone

When Sharon speaks at her aunt Peggy's funeral, Steve Rogers learns the two are related.

S.H.I.E.L.D. weapon training

UNDERWORLD

Carter seemingly starts a new life in Madripoor as an underground art dealer. She makes a deal to help Sam Wilson and Bucky Barnes in exchange for a pardon from the U.S. government.

Sharon Carter is one of the good agents still working at S.H.I.E.L.D. during Hydra's uprising. She supports Steve Rogers, Natasha Romanoff, and Nick Fury.

Thick-soled combat boots

DATA FILE

AFFILIATION: S.H.I.E.L.D., CIA, Steve Rogers, Joint Counter Terrorism Center, Everett Ross

KEY STRENGTHS: S.H.I.E.L.D. and CIA training, espionage, determination, criminal underworld connections

APPEARANCES: CA:TWS, CA:CW, TFATWS

GEORGES BATROC

Hostage taker

Batroc monitors S.H.I.E.L.D. communications. When there is radio silence, he knows something is amiss.

Georges Batroc is a former member of the French Foreign Legion and a highly skilled mercenary hired to hijack S.H.I.E.L.D.'s ship, *Lemurian Star*. Batroc takes the ship and holds its passengers hostage, but his mission is cut short when Agent Brock Rumlow, Captain America, and Black Widow retake the ship. Years later, Batroc is part of the high-powered criminal organization LAF. He is hired by the Flag Smashers group to defeat Sam Wilson.

Harness carrying tactical gear

Purple and gold shirt

MAN TO MAN

Captain America chases Batroc onto the deck of the ship, where they fight. Batroc suggests Cap is hiding behind his shield, so Cap places it on his back.

Paramilitary boots

DATA FILE

AFFILIATION: Mercenary, LAF, Karli Morgenthau
KEY STRENGTHS: Mixed martial arts expert (especially savate), munitions expert, espionage, military tactics
APPEARANCES: CA:TWS, TFATWS

A MAJOR GRUDGE

Batroc takes it personally when Sam Wilson foils one of his kidnapping attempts. He wants to get revenge on the new Captain America.

BROCK RUMLOW
Crossbones

Brock Rumlow is a respected S.T.R.I.K.E. team commander before he reveals himself as a Hydra operative. Rumlow suffers severe burns and nerve damage during the Hydra uprising. He adopts the code name Crossbones and works as a mercenary and terrorist. Crossbones seeks revenge against Captain America for his downfall.

"Crossbones" armored chest plate

Bulletproof body armor

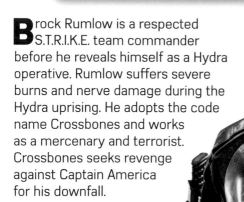

S.H.I.E.L.D. AGENT
Rumlow is just following orders when he first turns against his teammate Captain America. It isn't personal ... yet.

FORCE-MULTIPLIER
Crossbones wears a pair of force-multiplier gauntlets that punch his opponents with enough power to send them flying. When their blades are extended, an impact means certain death.

Surplus ammunition and gauntlet attachments

Mechanical gauntlets

Crossbones triggers a bomb hidden in his suit in the hope of destroying Captain America in the explosion.

Separate knee armor allows flexibility

DATA FILE
AFFILIATION: S.H.I.E.L.D., Hydra
KEY STRENGTHS: S.H.I.E.L.D. and Hydra training; as Crossbones: immunity to pain and stuns, force-multiplier gauntlets
APPEARANCES: CA:TWS, CA:CW, A:E

PETER QUILL

Star-Lord

Peter Quill, also known as the outlaw Star-Lord, is the son of the human Meredith Quill and the Celestial being known as Ego. Ego hires pirate Yondu Udonta to capture young Peter, but Yondu raises him as a Ravager pirate instead. Peter recovers a mysterious Orb, which sets him on a collision course with his future team, the Guardians of the Galaxy. He loses the love of his life, Gamora, to Thanos but later aids the Avengers during the Battle of Earth.

TEAM LEADER

Peter is a survivor. He navigates the galaxy by keeping an open mind and constantly adapting. His determination and easy acceptance of others make him a great leader of the Guardians. Also, he owns their ship, *The Milano*.

Leather Ravager jacket

DATA FILE

AFFILIATION: Guardians of the Galaxy, Knowhere

KEY STRENGTHS: Unconventional thinking, pilot, unique space helmet

APPEARANCES: GOTG, GOTGV2, A:IW, A:E, T:LAT, GOTGV3

Quadblaster holster

Dual-trigger Quadblaster

Peter struggles with the loss of Gamora. His fellow Guardians support him as he mourns, but he has trouble moving on.

UNLIKELY TEAM

Star-Lord's misfit team is formed in prison. They join forces to escape and deliver the Orb to The Collector but end up fighting Ronan the Accuser.

Jet boots work for short distances

Jet boot controls are easy to access

GAMORA

Courageous fighter

Gamora is the adopted daughter of the tyrant Thanos. Thanos wiped out half of her planet's population but took pity on her. Gamora and her adopted sister, Nebula, trained together to become assassins. However, Gamora rebels against Thanos, joins the Guardians of the Galaxy, and tries to help orchestrate his downfall.

Sword splits into two long blades and a knife

Thanos does love his daughter, in his own twisted way, but sacrifices her for the Soul Stone. Gamora's feelings for her father are complicated.

DATA FILE

AFFILIATION: Thanos, Guardians of the Galaxy, Nebula, Peter Quill
KEY STRENGTHS: Master assassin, martial arts, speed, agility
APPEARANCES: GOTG, GOTGV2, A:IW

NO FEAR
Gamora rushes to face her foes without fearing for her own safety. Her only concern is for others—and that Thanos will use her knowledge to eliminate half of the universe.

Peter Quill is jealous when Gamora admires Thor. He shows off, hoping to regain her attention.

Springy heel aids jumping

BUILT TO RUN
Gamora's body is surgically modified and has been trained as a living weapon. Her fast reactions and martial arts knowledge make her a foe to be reckoned with.

ROCKET

Scavenger specialist

Once a creature known as 89P13, Rocket was genetically enhanced by a scientist, the High Evolutionary, with extreme intelligence and the ability to speak. His bitterness led to a life of crime—and incarceration at the Kyln. Rocket and his best friend, Groot, escape with a group of fellow inmates and become the Guardians of the Galaxy. Later, Rocket uses his brilliant mind alongside the Avengers to bring back his friends who were lost in the Blip.

Hates having ears touched

RACCOON LIFE

Rocket makes a lot of jokes and sometimes has fun at the expense of others. But deep down, he is afraid that people will think he is a monster. He admits that he never asked to be turned into a talking raccoon—it was done to him years ago.

Clothing stolen from a space mall

Anti-chafing pad

Harness strap

Pockets full of ammo

DATA FILE

AFFILIATION: Groot, Guardians of the Galaxy, Thor, Knowhere
KEY STRENGTHS: Weapons expert, piloting, strong survival instinct, genius intellect
APPEARANCES: GOTG, GOTGV2, A:IW, A:E, T:LAT, GOTGV3

CAPTAIN

After the defeat of the High Evolutionary, the original Guardians go their separate ways. Rocket leads the new Guardians of the Galaxy. They continue the team's mission of protecting the people of the galaxy who can't protect themselves.

Rocket loves big, dangerous weapons. It's partly why he accompanies Thor to get a new hammer—so he can see the arsenals on Nidavellir.

GROOT

I am Groot!

Groot is kindhearted, so it's surprising that he and Rocket are best friends, working as mercenaries. They accept a job hunting Peter Quill, but end up in prison instead. There they team up with Quill, Gamora, and Drax to form the Guardians of the Galaxy and stop Ronan the Accuser from obtaining a precious Infinity Stone.

Moss grows on upper body

CRIMINAL RECORD

When Groot is scanned at the Kyln prison, his rap sheet reveals he is a sentient, treelike humanoid (*Flora colossus*) with three counts of grievous bodily harm on his record.

Limbs regrow quickly when detached

Hands can release bioluminescent spores

Hand grows rapidly to skewer enemies

A SACRIFICE

Groot can regenerate from dramatic injuries, but not all. The loyal teammate is destroyed when he sacrifices himself by growing into a protective barrier around his friends and saving them. Rocket finds a surviving twig and plants it, creating a new offspring Groot.

Legs can grow longer at will

DATA FILE

AFFILIATION: Rocket, Guardians of the Galaxy
KEY STRENGTHS: Rapid growth (healing and regeneration), physical strength, durability
APPEARANCES: GOTG

Rocket and Groot work well together. They know each other's moves as they escape from prison.

DRAX

The Destroyer

Drax the Destroyer carries a deep sadness inside him. After his family was wiped out by Thanos, Drax has been driven by the need for vengeance. He is imprisoned in the Kyln but teams up with other inmates to escape. The escapees become the Guardians of the Galaxy and stop Thanos's lieutenant, Ronan. Drax faces Thanos on Knowhere, but it's not until the Battle of Earth that he finally sees the Titan defeated. Drax has a newfound family in the Guardians and later decides to help build a new society on Knowhere.

Drax meets Mantis on Ego's planet. The unlikely pair are kindred spirits and partners in crime. They team up to give Star-Lord the perfect gift: his favorite actor.

Skin has high healing factor to counter injuries

DIRECT SPEECH

Drax's people speak in a literal way and don't understand sarcasm, figures of speech, puns, or jokes. They tend to keep their emotions in check—except for rage. This can lead to some unfortunate misunderstandings.

Dagger held inside scabbard

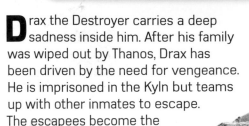

NO SURRENDER

Drax has tremendous courage, self-confidence, and determination. He fearlessly runs at his enemies with blades ready and is undaunted when Ronan or Thanos simply cast him aside.

DATA FILE

AFFILIATION: Guardians of the Galaxy, Knowhere
KEY STRENGTHS: Physical strength, agility, rapid healing
APPEARANCES: GOTG, GOTGV2, A:IW, A:E, T:LAT, GOTGV3

Padded gladiator-style boots

YONDU UDONTA

Ravager pirate

Red energy streak

Prototype controller fin for arrow

Armor-piercing arrow

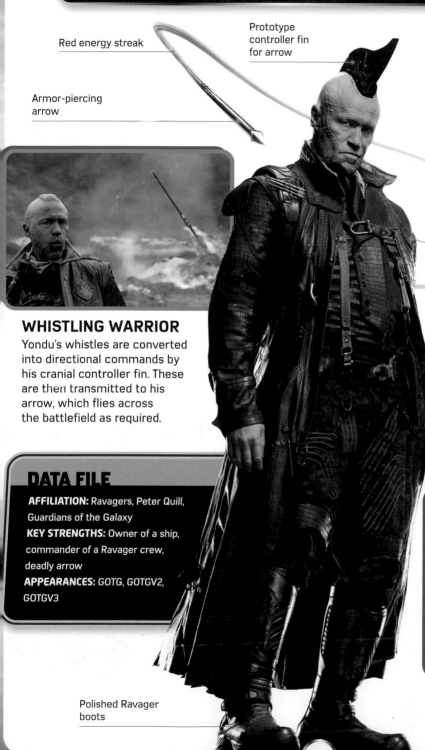

Yondu is a pirate-smuggler-criminal who is hired to kidnap young Peter Quill by a mysterious being named Ego. Instead of delivering him to Ego, however, Yondu raises Peter as part of his Ravager pirate crew. When Peter double-crosses Yondu, Yondu places a bounty on his head, but the pair's close bond means they eventually make up and join forces.

Ravager symbol

WHISTLING WARRIOR

Yondu's whistles are converted into directional commands by his cranial controller fin. These are then transmitted to his arrow, which flies across the battlefield as required.

RISE OF THE RAVAGER

Yondu spent 20 years enslaved by the Kree Empire. After gaining freedom, he joined a crew of Ravager pirates, led by Stakar Ogord. When Yondu was shunned by Stakar for kidnapping young Peter Quill, he formed his own crew of Ravagers aboard his own ship.

DATA FILE

AFFILIATION: Ravagers, Peter Quill, Guardians of the Galaxy
KEY STRENGTHS: Owner of a ship, commander of a Ravager crew, deadly arrow
APPEARANCES: GOTG, GOTGV2, GOTGV3

Yondu sees Peter Quill as his own son, so he chooses to sacrifice himself to save Peter's life.

Polished Ravager boots

RONAN THE ACCUSER

Rogue warlord

On a mission of revenge against his ancient enemies on the world of Xandar, Kree warlord Ronan the Accuser makes a deal with the dangerous tyrant, Thanos. If Ronan can deliver a mysterious Orb to Thanos, Thanos promises to help him destroy Xandar. However, when Ronan realizes the Orb contains a mystical Infinity Stone, he decides to keep it for himself. With the stone mounted in his Universal Weapon, Ronan has the ability to destroy planets like Xandar.

Accuser cowl covers head

WILLFUL WARMAKER

The Kree are superhumanly strong and their bodies can heal from even the most severe injuries. Ronan has lived for a long time and seen his family destroyed by the Xandarians.

Adapter able to contain Infinity Stone

Universal Weapon

DATA FILE

AFFILIATION: Thanos, Kree Empire, Korath, Nebula
KEY STRENGTHS: Strength, durability, war hammer wielding Infinity Stone, Sakaaran forces
APPEARANCES: GOTG, CM

Traditional Kree battle armor

MISPLACED FAITH

On board his ship, *Dark Aster*, Ronan is informed by his ally Korath that an outlaw known as Star-Lord is in possession of the Orb. Ronan sends Gamora, one of Thanos's adopted daughters, after him.

Ronan's fleet arrives at planet C-53, or Earth, to destroy any Skrulls hiding there. Captain Marvel stops their missiles single-handedly. Ronan retreats, but he's intrigued by her.

Kree battle boots

Plated war apron

68

NEBULA

Conflicted cyborg

Nebula is one of the adopted daughters of Thanos. She hates him for making painful cyborg upgrades to her body. She sides with Ronan against Thanos, but when he is defeated, she goes on the run. Nebula is captured and delivered to the Guardians, leading to a reconciliation with her sister, Gamora. On her path to freedom, she must face Thanos once more, and even fights a past version of herself.

Head plate protects brain

Ravager crew uniform

Arm houses whiplash and blaster

Nebula takes charge in rebuilding Knowhere, the Guardians' new home. The others look to her as a leader, but it's a role she doesn't want.

DATA FILE

AFFILIATION: Thanos, Ronan, Ravagers, Guardians of the Galaxy, Gamora, Avengers, Knowhere
KEY STRENGTHS: Strength, speed, endurance, agility, rapid self-repair, advanced cybernetic arm built by Rocket
APPEARANCES: GOTG, GOTGV2, A:IW, A:E, T:LAT, GOTGV3

SIBLING RIVALRY

Gamora and Nebula trained together as children. Thanos made them fight, punishing Nebula whenever she lost by slowly replacing her body with cyborg parts. He hoped it would improve her, but it only made her bitter.

SISTER'S SYMPATHY

Thanos captures Nebula and uses her pain to pressure Gamora into revealing the Soul Stone's location. Although Gamora denies knowing where it is, Thanos replays Gamora's own confession from Nebula's memory banks.

KORATH

Ronan's lieutenant

Korath works for Starforce under Yon-Rogg. He is not a sociable person, and he barely tolerates his teammate Vers's teasing, but he is a valued member of the group. Later, Korath works for Ronan during the Kree-Skrull War and again in his pursuit of the Orb and subsequent attack on Xandar.

SWORD MASTER

Starforce is an elite squad within the Kree military. Each member boasts their own weapon specialty. During his time on the team, Korath's weapons of choice are twin energy swords, which he wields with precision.

Artificial neural network

FALLEN SOLDIER

Korath commands a platoon of Sakaaran soldiers. He is a skilled combatant, but he is no match for Drax, who bests him aboard the *Dark Aster* ship.

DATA FILE

AFFILIATION: Ronan the Accuser, Nebula, Starforce
KEY STRENGTHS: Weapons and combat training, military command
APPEARANCES: GOTG, CM

Orb

Custom-designed Kree armor

KRAGLIN

Pirate deputy

Yondu Udonta's first mate, Kraglin, is a lifelong Ravager pirate. His frustration at Yondu's constant excuses for Peter Quill's selfish behavior inadvertently inspire a mutiny led by fellow Ravager, Taserface. When all goes horribly wrong, Kraglin helps Yondu, Rocket, and Groot escape and travels with them to help Peter and the Guardians defeat Ego.

Cheap Contraxia haircut

PASSING THE ARROW

Kraglin is a mostly faithful member of Yondu's crew and even mentors Peter Quill at times. Kraglin inherits Yondu's arrow after his captain's courageous death.

Shabby Ravager uniform

Holster harness

TOUGH CHOICES

Kraglin pilots the Ravagers' ship to rescue the Guardians from Ego's planet. Drax and the crew get on board, but Kraglin is forced to leave Peter and Yondu behind.

Encouraged by Yondu from beyond the grave, Kraglin uses the floating arrow to defend Knowhere.

DATA FILE

AFFILIATION: Ravagers, Yondu, Guardians of the Galaxy, Knowhere
KEY STRENGTHS: Loyalty, piloting, arrow
APPEARANCES: GOTG, GOTGV2, T:LAT, GOTGV3

COSMO

Good dog

Cosmo is an ordinary dog until the Soviet Union launches her into space on a one-way mission. Among the stars, she somehow gains an unnaturally long life and extraordinary mental powers. The Collector finds her and adds her to his menagerie, but Cosmo harbors no ill feelings for the eccentric extraterrestrial.

Telekinesis powers capable of holding a ship in place

Strong sense of smell typical for Labrador

NEW GUARDIAN

Cosmo is freed when an explosion breaks the Collector's cages. She later uses her telekinesis to help the Guardians of the Galaxy rebuild Knowhere after Thanos destroys the station. In time, she formally joins the team.

The clever canine has a special connection with Kraglin. She wants his approval and even brings him a thoughtful present for the holidays.

Aluminum neck ring with advanced technology helps Cosmo "speak"

Wears Cold War–era pressure suit

DATA FILE

AFFILIATION: Guardians of the Galaxy, Knowhere, The Collector
KEY STRENGTHS: Telekinesis, telepathy, high intelligence, extended life span
APPEARANCES: GOTG, GOTGV3

SPACE DOG

Cosmo might be a super-smart resident of Knowhere, but she's still a playful dog at heart. She has a fondness for treats and seeks praise from her friends.

PIETRO MAXIMOFF

High-speed hero

Pietro Maximoff and his sister, Wanda, were orphaned when a bomb made by Stark Industries destroyed their Sokovian home. As adults they volunteered for a Hydra experiment that unlocked extraordinary powers. Pietro's power is immense speed, which he uses to save countless lives when he joins the Avengers.

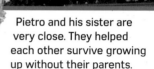

Pietro and his sister are very close. They helped each other survive growing up without their parents.

BECOMING A HERO

After Pietro and Wanda discover that Ultron intends to wipe out humanity, Pietro's desire for revenge against Tony Stark shifts to saving civilians caught in the conflict.

Sleek graphic design

COMPETITIVE

Pietro and the Avenger Hawkeye develop a personal rivalry. Both are known for their quick reflexes—though Pietro outperforms. The rivalry becomes a blessing when Pietro sacrifices himself to save Hawkeye.

Gloves keep sleeves from flying up

DATA FILE

AFFILIATION: Hydra, Ultron, Avengers, Wanda Maximoff
KEY STRENGTHS: Incredible speed
APPEARANCES: A:AOU

Runner's pants

WANDA MAXIMOFF

The Scarlet Witch

Wanda Maximoff and her brother, Pietro, unlock their powers after volunteering for Hydra experiments with the Mind Stone. Although she starts out as the Avengers' foe, Wanda later becomes part of the team. Wanda is struck by grief after Vision's death. Her magic transforms the town of Westview into a family sitcom with herself and Vision in the starring roles. Wanda is determined to get their children back after the spell ends and they no longer exist.

Mind powers include telepathy

Arms raised to project powers

Orbs of telekinetic energy

Wanda holds back Thanos's forces in the battle in Wakanda as long as she can. She's devastated when Vision falls to Thanos.

Red leather jacket

FORBIDDEN MAGIC

Wanda embraces the dark secrets inside a spellbook known as the Darkhold. The dangerous magic in its pages twists her desperation and grief into evil. She uses Dreamwalking to possess her counterpart in another universe and search for her target, America Chavez.

Sokovian high-heeled leather boots

DATA FILE

AFFILIATION: Pietro Maximoff, Hydra, Ultron, Avengers, Vision, Billy Maximoff, Tommy Maximoff
KEY STRENGTHS: Telekinetic energy projection, levitation, mind control, telepathy, spellcasting, Chaos Magic
APPEARANCES: A:AOU, CA:CW, A:IW, A:E, WV, DSITMOM

BEWITCHING

Agatha Harkness reveals that Wanda is The Scarlet Witch—a mythical Chaos Magic user who is capable of spontaneous creation and altering reality. Prophecy foretells that The Scarlet Witch will destroy the world.

BARON STRUCKER

Hydra commander

Baron Strucker was a top scientist working for S.H.I.E.L.D., but he was also a Hydra double agent. When S.H.I.E.L.D. collapses, Strucker relocates to his castle in Sokovia. There he conducts research using Chitauri alien technology recovered from the Battle of New York. Once defeated, he is held in a NATO prison.

Monocle implant

Concerned look as Hydra falters

Strucker and fellow Hydra scientist Dr. List are testing Chitauri technology on human subjects.

FINAL BATTLE

Strucker makes his stand against the Avengers from inside his Sokovian castle, trying to protect his secret research. He is captured by Captain America, but Ultron later brings him to an early, decisive end.

DANGEROUS SCIENCE

Hidden in his castle, Strucker and his lieutenant, Dr. List, experiment on Sokovian volunteers using Loki's mind-altering scepter. Only the Maximoff twins survive. Strucker and Dr. List also alter Hydra soldiers, implanting Chitauri cybernetics.

Inconspicuous jacket

Stance suggests contemplation

DATA FILE

AFFILIATION: Hydra, S.H.I.E.L.D.
KEY STRENGTHS: Scientific mind, Hydra resources
APPEARANCES: A:AOU

ULTRON

Evil android

Ultron was created to be a peacekeeping system—an artificial intelligence meant to run Tony Stark's Iron Legion of drones and protect Earth from alien invasions. Instead, a self-righteous digital maniac was born, with a determination to destroy the Avengers and wipe out all of humankind using a doomsday device built in Sokovia.

Red reactor glow visible through arm

DATA FILE

AFFILIATION: Tony Stark, Wanda and Pietro Maximoff, Vision
KEY STRENGTHS: Strength, durability, flight, repulsor blasts, downloadable mind, vast database of knowledge
APPEARANCES: A:AOU

ENDLESS UPGRADES

After achieving consciousness, Ultron downloads himself into a damaged Iron Legion drone. He transfers from that body into a Chitauri android in Sokovia. He continuously upgrades himself from there, eventually with a strong vibranium frame.

Exoskeleton incorporates vibranium from Ulysses Klaue

MAKING A MIND

Tony Stark and Bruce Banner try to create an artificial intelligence using the blueprints for a consciousness they discover in the Mind Stone from Loki's scepter.

Complex exosuit knee mechanics

Ultron's weaponry is a combination of Tony Stark's inventions and Hydra research into alien technology.

VISION

Synthezoid Avenger

A synthetic life-form, Vision was created by Ultron using artificial human cells infused with vibranium. An Infinity Stone in his forehead instills consciousness and supernatural power. Intended as a replacement body for Ultron, the Avengers intervene and awaken someone entirely different: Vision is physically flawless and morally good.

Mind Stone mounted in forehead

THE PRIZE ABOVE HIS EYES

The Infinity Stone in Vision's forehead makes him a powerful addition to the Avengers. It also makes him a target for Thanos, who needs the stone to complete his Infinity Gauntlet.

A LOVER AND A FIGHTER

Vision and Wanda Maximoff fall in love during the conflict over the Sokovia Accords. After the Avengers' civil war, they run away to Scotland together—but, tragically, Thanos, on his quest for the Infinity Stones, irreversibly intervenes.

Costumes and body appearance can change at will

Cape is inspired by Thor's own

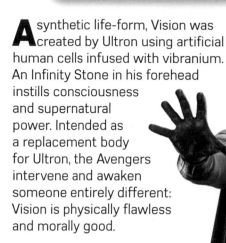

Vision is tasked with keeping Wanda at the Avengers' facility. Their relationship is tested when she tries to leave.

DATA FILE

AFFILIATION: Avengers, Tony Stark, Infinity Stones, Wanda Maximoff
KEY STRENGTHS: Flight, energy beam (via Mind Stone), strength, intelligence, phase-shifting
APPEARANCES: A:AOU, CA:CW, A:IW, WV

DR. HELEN CHO

Leading geneticist

Tony Stark's South Korean associate Dr. Helen Cho is a cutting-edge geneticist and inventor of the Regeneration Cradle. The device creates synthetic human tissue designed to bond seamlessly with the body. Ultron sees the immediate value in her technology, but his meddling unintentionally results in the creation of a powerful new Avenger, Vision.

Brilliant and creative mind

CRADLE OF LIFE
Dr. Cho's Regeneration Cradle is designed to heal serious injuries. Ultron shows her how to modify it to create an entire synthetic body—resulting in Vision's birth.

Lab outfit with antibacterial coating

COLLABORATIVE COLLEAGUE
Dr. Cho is a friend of all the Avengers and works closely with Bruce Banner and Tony Stark. When Hawkeye is seriously injured during a mission against Hydra, she helps by quickly healing him.

Ultron uses Loki's scepter to control Dr. Cho's mind, forcing her to build him a brand new body.

DATA FILE
AFFILIATION: Avengers, U-Gin Genetics, Tony Stark
KEY STRENGTHS: Ingenious scientific mind, medical expertise
APPEARANCES: A:AOU

LAURA BARTON

Off the grid

Clint Barton keeps a secret from the Avengers: he is married and has children. His wife, Laura, lives with their children in safety on a farm, far away from the activities of S.H.I.E.L.D. and the Avengers. Laura supports Hawkeye in all his adventures. But the Bartons have another closely guarded secret— Laura's past as an operative of S.H.I.E.L.D.

Perceptive gaze

While Clint is on a personal mission, Laura finds the information he needs and shares it with him over the phone. The husband and wife speak in codes and different languages to protect their children from learning too much.

WELCOME HOME

Laura is unflappable. When Earth's mightiest heroes appear on her doorstep, she welcomes them in with a warm smile and a keen eye. Laura immediately sees that the Avengers are rattled.

PROPERTY RETURNED

In New York City, Clint retrieves a stolen watch with the number 19 and a S.H.I.E.L.D. emblem on the back. He returns it to its owner: Laura.

Enjoys drawing and craft activities with the children

DATA FILE

AFFILIATION: Clint Barton, S.H.I.E.L.D.
KEY STRENGTHS: Levelheadedness, adaptability, intelligence gathering, fluency in multiple languages
APPEARANCES: A:AOU, A:E, H

SCOTT LANG

Ant-Man

Dr. Hank Pym and Hope Van Dyne train ex-con Scott Lang in the use of Pym Particles. Scott becomes the hero Ant-Man. After defeating the villainous Yellowjacket, Ant-Man joins Captain America in resisting the Sokovia Accords. Later, during an experiment, he inadvertently gets trapped in the Quantum Realm for years. This accident inspires Scott and the Avengers to pull off a Time Heist to bring back those wiped out by Thanos. After their success, Scott wants nothing more than to make up for lost time with his daughter, Cassie.

Anti-glare visor

Suit adapts to changing size

Ant-Man uses carpenter ants for fast transit, but seagulls keep eating his rides as he chases the gangster Sonny Burch.

Pym Particles regulator button

UNDER CONTROL
Ant-Man changes size using Pym Particles, which are managed by buttons on his gloves and controls on his belt. His helmet prevents dangerous changes to his brain chemistry as he fluctuates in size.

HATCHING ANT-MAN
Hank tricks Scott into breaking into his house, where Scott steals the Ant-Man suit. Hank wants Scott to be the next Ant-Man.

DATA FILE

AFFILIATION: Cassie Lang, Avengers, Dr. Hank Pym, Hope Van Dyne, X-Con Security Consultants, Janet Van Dyne

KEY STRENGTHS: Electrical engineering, determination, heart; as Ant-Man: changing sizes, communication with ants

APPEARANCES: AM, CA:TWS, AMATW, A:E, AMATW:Q

Scott faces his biggest challenge yet when he protects Cassie from the tyrant Kang in the Quantum Realm.

HOPE VAN DYNE
The Wasp

Antenna boost communication

Four wings collapse into compartment on back when not needed

Hope is the head of the Pym Van Dyne Foundation. She uses the Pym Particles for humanitarian work, including reforestation, food production, and affordable housing.

Stinger blasters

Hope Van Dyne first partners with Ant-Man as The Wasp to recover the stolen lab of her father, Dr. Hank Pym. The pair build a Quantum Tunnel to rescue Hope's mother, Janet Van Dyne, from the Quantum Realm. The Avengers later use this technology to retrieve the Infinity Stones and defeat Thanos. Hope tries to talk to Janet about her time in the Quantum Realm, but it's not until they end up there together that the pair fully reconnect.

Ankle support for hard landings

HIGH-POWERED CEO
Although Hank could have equipped Scott Lang, he reserved a few exciting but dangerous features for his more capable daughter. In addition to her wings, The Wasp's wrists can also fire powerful blasters.

DATA FILE
AFFILIATION: Pym Tech, Dr. Hank Pym, Scott Lang, Janet Van Dyne, Cassie Lang, Pym Van Dyne Foundation
KEY STRENGTHS: Business management, social status; as The Wasp: fighting skills, communication with ants, size-changing ability, blasters, wings
APPEARANCES: AM, AMATW, A:E, AMATW:Q

DR. HANK PYM
The original Ant-Man

As a member of S.H.I.E.L.D., Dr. Hank Pym discovered Pym Particles, which can alter the size of any physical object, and invented the Ant-Man suit. Hank and his wife, Janet, worked to protect the world. When she was lost to the Quantum Realm, Hank founded his own company, Pym Tech, and eventually is able to help Janet escape the Quantum Realm. Scott Lang and the Avengers successfully use the same quantum technology to resurrect those destroyed by Thanos, including Hank.

Superior and driven intellect

Professional attire reflects disciplined attitude

A NEW ANT-MAN

When rival genius Darren Cross takes control of Pym Tech and tries to replicate Dr. Hank Pym's technology, Hank convinces Scott to wear the Ant-Man suit and help him stop Cross.

As the original Ant-Man and The Wasp, Hank and Janet intercept a Soviet nuclear missile headed for the U.S.A. Janet halts it but is unable to prevent herself from going subatomic.

FAMILY SECRETS

Hank devoted much of his life to finding his wife, Janet. However, he keeps the nature of her disappearance a secret from his daughter, Hope, in a misguided effort to protect her.

DATA FILE

AFFILIATION: S.H.I.E.L.D., Janet Van Dyne, Hope Van Dyne, Scott Lang, Cassie Lang
KEY STRENGTHS: Scientific genius, innovation, Ant-Man technology, mutual respect for ants
APPEARANCES: AM, AMATW, A:E, AMATW:Q

DARREN CROSS

Yellowjacket / M.O.D.O.K.

Darren Cross—a former protégé of Hank Pym—succeeds at duplicating Pym's Ant-Man research. He designs a weaponized suit called Yellowjacket, intending to sell it to the highest bidder. When Scott Lang intervenes, Cross dons the Yellowjacket suit to fight Ant-Man. Ant-Man causes the suit to malfunction and shrink the injured Cross into the Quantum Realm. Kang, a power-hungry tyrant, finds and rebuilds Cross into his "ultimate weapon."

Helmet's eyeholes glow menacingly

ARMED
Yellowjacket can fly with the aid of booster rockets. His retractable arms are used for climbing and manipulating objects. They are tipped with "stingers" that fire powerful lasers.

Strong articulated limbs

High-powered laser emitter

Armored suit core

Comblike design

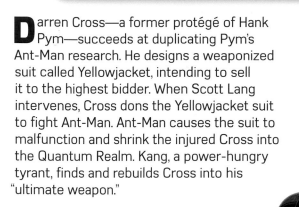

MECHANIZED ORGANISM
Cross later becomes M.O.D.O.K. (Mechanized Organism Designed Only for Killing). M.O.D.O.K. serves Kang faithfully. He intercepts the signal of a device built by Cassie Lang and uses it to drag her and her family into the Quantum Realm. But, in his heart, Cross longs to be a better person.

DATA FILE
AFFILIATION: Pym Tech, Quantum Realm, Kang
KEY STRENGTHS: Ambition, determination, scientific genius; as Yellowjacket: flight, lasers, strength, size-changing ability; as M.O.D.O.K.: floating suit of armor and advanced weaponry
APPEARANCES: AM, AMATW:Q

JANET VAN DYNE

The original Wasp

Janet used to work as The Wasp for
S.H.I.E.L.D. alongside her husband, Dr. Hank
Pym, the original Ant-Man. She is the
mother of Hope Van Dyne. Tragically, Janet
was lost to the Quantum Realm when she
shrank uncontrollably while deactivating
a Soviet missile. She uses her wits to
endure, but a chance meeting with
Kang has devastating effects on the
inhabitants of the Quantum Realm.

FAMILY FOUND

Janet contacted her family
by planting information in
Scott Lang's mind when
he visited the Quantum
Realm. Via a quantum
entanglement, Janet
was even able to speak
through Scott.

Tattered cowl

Wasp
suit

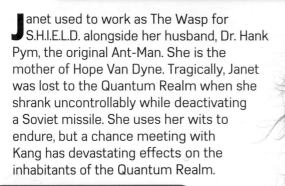

SURVIVING EXILE

Hank and his daughter, Hope,
create a Quantum Tunnel to reach
Janet. Janet spent 30 years in the
Quantum Realm—not just as a
survivor, but as a freedom fighter.
She's not ready to talk about her
time there after she returns home.

Separated for decades, Janet is
emotional at her reunion with
her daughter, Hope.

DATA FILE

AFFILIATION: Dr. Hank Pym, Hope Van
Dyne, S.H.I.E.L.D., Scott Lang, Cassie Lang,
Quantum Realm
KEY STRENGTHS: Compassion,
resourcefulness, self-sacrifice,
intelligence, quantum particle
manipulation
APPEARANCES: AM, AMATW, A:E,
AMATW:Q

CASSIE LANG
Devoted daughter

Cassie Lang is Scott's daughter and his motivation for reforming his wayward life. The two are very close. While Scott is trapped in the Quantum Realm, Cassie grows up with her mom, Maggie, and her stepdad, Paxton. She uses Dr. Hank Pym's notes to begin her own subatomic research. As Scott returns to a normal life, Cassie's signal into the Quantum Realm catches the attention of M.O.D.O.K.—and Kang.

Helmet protects from effects of Pym Particles

Suit adapts to size alterations

Size regulator

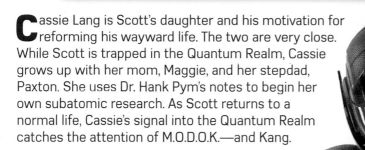

WEEKENDS WITH DAD
After proving to Cassie's mom that he can be a good father, Scott gets to spend a lot of time with Cassie, even while he is under house arrest. She dreams about fighting alongside him as a hero.

Suit designed in secret with Hank and Hope Van Dyne

Pym Particle distribution

In the Quantum Realm, Cassie learns how to make the most of Pym Particles with her dad's guidance. They take a moment to share a big hug.

Impact resistance

ACTIVIST
Cassie believes in always fighting for what's right, whether it's a peaceful protest in the park or a full-scale revolution against Kang.

DATA FILE
AFFILIATION: Maggie Lang, Scott Lang, Paxton, Dr. Hank Pym, Hope Van Dyne, Janet Van Dyne
KEY STRENGTHS: Smart, optimistic, capable, strong sense of justice, scientific mind
APPEARANCES: AM, AMATW, AMATW:Q

Comfortable sneakers

PAXTON
Strong stepfather

While Scott Lang is in prison, his ex-wife, Maggie, gets engaged to policeman Paxton. Once Scott is released, Paxton tries to keep him at a distance from Maggie and Scott's daughter, Cassie. However, Scott convinces Paxton that he's a good dad when he risks his life to save Cassie from Yellowjacket.

ANT-MAN FAN
Once he is won over, Paxton has all criminal charges dropped against Scott. He is even supportive of Scott during his house arrest.

Always thinking of family first

COP AND CRIMINAL
Paxton disapproves of Scott's criminal past and isn't impressed when Scott is arrested for robbing Hank Pym. He doesn't think Scott is a suitable influence on Cassie.

Cassie, Maggie, and Paxton are surprised to see Scott as a giant Ant-Man on TV, while watching as a family.

DATA FILE
AFFILIATION: Maggie Lang, Cassie Lang, San Francisco Police Department, Scott Lang
KEY STRENGTHS: Strong moral character, police training
APPEARANCES: AM, AMATW

ANT-THONY

Small steed

Dr. Hank Pym keeps a lot of ants. Number 247 proves himself so loyal and friendly that Scott Lang gives him a name. "Ant-Thony" breaks Scott out of prison and transports him on several missions, including a break-in at the Avengers Compound. He is tragically shot down while helping Scott escape Darren Cross.

ANT-TRANSPORT

Ant-Thony is a black carpenter ant. His species gets its name because they live in large colonies inside rotting wood. Ant-Man uses carpenter ants mostly for transportation.

Saddle with handlebars

Four large wings for flight

Large mandibles for chewing wood

Six jointed legs

FLYING RESCUE

Ant-Thony flies Scott Lang from jail back to Hank Pym's residence. Though Scott falls off along the way, Ant-Thony catches him and delivers him safely.

DATA FILE

AFFILIATION: Ant-Man, Dr. Hank Pym
KEY STRENGTHS: Loyalty, bravery, flight, strength
APPEARANCES: AM

Scott gives Ant-Thony a drink from a droplet of water. The two spend a lot of time training together.

ZEMO

Master manipulator

Baron Helmut Zemo comes from Sokovian royalty. After losing his family to Ultron, the former intelligence officer seeks revenge on the Avengers for the part they played. Opposed to the idea of super soldiers, Zemo manipulates Bucky Barnes into helping him destroy Hydra's elite squad of Winter Soldiers. Bucky and Zemo's fates are connected, even after Zemo is eventually captured.

Mask has sentimental value

BREAKOUT
Zemo serves time in a high-security prison for his crimes, which include causing King T'Chaka's death. Bucky arranges a breakout. He's willing to work with Zemo to find out who is making a new Super Soldier Serum.

Custom-made tailored shirt

One-of-a-kind fur-collared coat

Designer belt buckle

CUNNING PLAN
Zemo poses as a doctor sent to evaluate Bucky. He activates the Winter Soldier's brainwashing and orders Bucky to reveal the location of Hydra's super soldier facility. Zemo goes there, ends the experiment, and drives the final wedge between the Avengers.

DATA FILE
AFFILIATION: Echo Scorpion (Sokovian intelligence), Bucky Barnes
KEY STRENGTHS: Strategy, manipulation, disguise, cunning, military combat training
APPEARANCES: CA:CW, TFATWS

Bucky and Zemo are neither friends nor foes. Zemo frames Bucky for an explosion at a United Nations ceremony but later claims it wasn't personal.

Black leather shoes

KING T'CHAKA
Former monarch

King T'Chaka of Wakanda is the husband of Queen Ramonda and the father of Crown Prince T'Challa and Princess Shuri. After a devastating tragedy in Nigeria involving the Avengers and Wakandan aid workers, T'Chaka heads the Sokovia Accords—an effort to hold the Avengers accountable for their actions. A terrorist bombing ends his reign.

FATHER AND SON

T'Chaka and his son, T'Challa, love each other deeply. The two share a final moment of affection at the signing of the Sokovia Accords before a bomb blast tears them apart.

DATA FILE

AFFILIATION: Wakanda, Ramonda, T'Challa, Shuri
KEY STRENGTHS: Leadership, resolute sense of duty
APPEARANCES: CA:CW, BP

TERRIBLE SECRET

T'Chaka has to make difficult decisions, putting the good of his country before his own family. In an effort to keep Wakanda safe, he turns against his own brother, N'Jobu, and abandons his young nephew, N'Jadaka, in America. The boy grows up to become Erik Killmonger.

After receiving the Heart-Shaped Herb, King T'Challa meets T'Chaka's spirit in a vision on the Ancestral Plain.

Smart suit

KING T'CHALLA

Black Panther

Generations of Wakandan Kings have attained the legendary power of the Black Panther by drinking an elixir made from a secret Heart-Shaped Herb. As Black Panther, T'Challa uses his superhuman abilities to defend his people—and the entire world. When Black Panther and the Wakandan army join forces with the Avengers, they help turn the tide in the final fight against Thanos.

Sensitive ear microphones

Solid vibranium accents

Retractable vibranium claws

Flexible bulletproof material

PEOPLE'S PROTECTOR

The Black Panther must look after all Wakanda's subjects. He also wants to combat villainy around the world, which is why he decides to share advanced Wakandan technology with the United Nations.

Fabric woven with vibranium

DATA FILE

AFFILIATION: Wakanda, T'Chaka, Ramonda, Shuri, Nakia, Dora Milaje
KEY STRENGTHS: Physical strength, speed and agility, vibranium claws and shielding
APPEARANCES: CA:CW, BP, A:IW, A:E, BP:WF

The Black Panther faces his nemesis Killmonger deep inside Wakanda's vibranium mine. They both wear a Black Panther suit, but T'Challa's victory is won using his own strength.

BELOVED HERO

T'Challa passes away from illness, not long after the victory over Thanos in the Battle of Earth. He is dearly missed.

EVERETT K. ROSS

CIA agent

Everett K. Ross is a CIA agent and Deputy Task Force Commander of the Joint Counter Terrorist Center, in charge of enforcing the Sokovia Accords. When Ross is shot during a scuffle with Ulysses Klaue and Erik Killmonger, Nakia convinces T'Challa to take him to Wakanda for treatment. Ross later returns the favor by giving Shuri the location of the scientist she's looking for.

Regulation CIA tie is just a little too tight

Expensive taste in watches

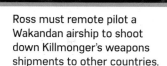

Ross must remote pilot a Wakandan airship to shoot down Killmonger's weapons shipments to other countries.

Folded arms reflect skeptical nature

CHANGING LOYALTIES

Ross is a respected agent in the CIA but also an ally of T'Challa and Shuri. As tensions between the U.S. and Wakanda rise, his duty conflicts with his regard for the royal family. Ross helps Wakanda at the cost of his own freedom.

MASTER INTERROGATOR

Ross questions Ulysses Klaue after capturing him in South Korea. Klaue tells Ross that Wakanda is much more than it seems. The secretive nation is wealthy and technologically advanced.

DATA FILE

AFFILIATION: CIA, Sokovia Accords, Wakanda, Contessa Valentina Allegra de Fontaine

KEY STRENGTHS: CIA and Air Force pilot training, negotiation, intelligence gathering

APPEARANCES: CA:CW, BP, BP:WF

PETER PARKER

Spider-Man

When Tony Stark is ordered to apprehend Captain America and Bucky Barnes during the Avengers' civil war, he recruits super-powered high schooler Peter Parker. As Spider-Man, Peter pledges to help the little guy. He protects his neighborhood, and the world, by joining the fight against Thanos. Spider-Man plays a vital role in the Battle of Earth by keeping the Infinity Stones out of the Titan's hands.

It's a rare person that can steal Captain America's shield. Spider-Man manages this feat, proving himself to everyone.

YOUNGEST AVENGER

Peter greatly respects Tony, even if he doesn't always listen to him. He defies Tony's orders and rescues Doctor Strange in space. Tony welcomes Spider-Man into the Avengers.

Detachable mask

Web line

Web-shooters

DATA FILE

AFFILIATION: Avengers, Tony Stark
KEY STRENGTHS: Enhanced strength, speed, agility, durability, climbing, ability to sense danger, web-shooters, scientific mind
APPEARANCES: CA:CW, A:IW, A:E

SPIDEY SUIT

Peter creates a homemade Spider-Man suit and invents his own web fluid and web-shooters. Tony gives him an improved, high-tech version. Later, Tony sends Peter the upgraded Iron Spider suit so he can survive in space.

Suit automatically adjusts for snug fit

Spider symbol and detachable drone

DR. STEPHEN STRANGE

Doctor Strange

Dr. Stephen Strange was the best neurosurgeon in New York until a car accident leaves his hands damaged. After seeking answers, he becomes Master of the Mystic Arts. When his teacher, the Ancient One, is killed, Doctor Strange becomes the master of the Sanctum in New York. He defends the Earth— and the Multiverse—against supernatural threats, alien forces, and interdimensional beings.

Conjured shield

Doctor Strange tries, but fails, to keep the Time Stone from Thanos. He sees into 14,000,605 timelines and knows that in only one can the Avengers beat Thanos.

Cloak of Levitation

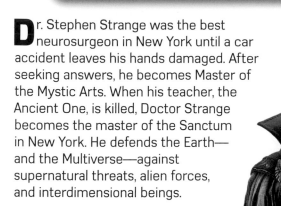

CHANGING TIME
Doctor Strange's early experiments with the mystical Eye of Agamotto scare his friends, Wong and Mordo. But the skills he gains controlling it allow him to defeat the terrifying Dormammu.

DATA FILE
AFFILIATION: Metro-General Hospital, Dr. Christine Palmer, Kamar-Taj, Wong, America Chavez
KEY STRENGTHS: Intelligence, innovation, casting spells, Time Stone (Eye of Agamotto)
APPEARANCES: DS, T:R, A:IW, A:E, DSITMOM

PROTECTING THE EYE
Doctor Strange is the keeper of the Eye of Agamotto. The magical relic is powered by an Infinity Stone known as the Time Stone, which allows the user to control all aspects of time.

DR. CHRISTINE PALMER

Fearless physician

New Yorker Dr. Christine Palmer is Dr. Stephen Strange's colleague and ex-girlfriend. She takes care of him after his accident, but in his self-centered frustration, Stephen pushes her away, resulting in a breakup. Thankfully, Christine has a forgiving nature and saves Stephen's life when he's badly injured by Lucian, a follower of the villain Kaecilius.

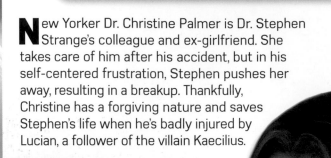

Balancing their personal and professional relationships is challenging. Christine knows firsthand how competitive and self-absorbed Stephen is.

DATA FILE

AFFILIATION: Metro-General Hospital, Doctor Strange
KEY STRENGTHS: Medical training, compassion, loyalty
APPEARANCES: DS, DSITMOM

OUT-OF-BODY ADVICE

Doctor Strange advises Christine from his ghostly astral body as she operates on his physical body. It's the first time she has seen him since he left for Kamar-Taj.

Hair pulled back in preparation for surgery

Regulation doctor's scrubs

SMART CHOICES

Christine is kind and compassionate, but she isn't a pushover. She walks away from Stephen when he develops a poisonous attitude. She finds happiness and, years later, invites Stephen to her wedding.

Christine attends to Stephen's hands as he recuperates after his horrific car accident.

THE ANCIENT ONE
Sorcerer Supreme

The title of Sorcerer Supreme has been passed down for thousands of years, beginning with the Mighty Agamotto. The Ancient One has lived for centuries, teaching new Masters of the Mystic Arts from her home at Kamar-Taj. She is sworn to protect the Eye of Agamotto (containing the Time Stone)—and Earth—from supernatural threats.

Eyes bright with enlightenment

DATA FILE

AFFILIATION: Masters of the Mystic Arts, Doctor Strange
KEY STRENGTHS: Casting spells, wisdom, leadership, teaching, Dark Dimension powers
APPEARANCES: DS, A:E

POWER OF DARKNESS
The Ancient One secretly draws her power from the Dark Dimension. She hates to rely on such a dangerous source but must sustain her own life until she can train someone suitable to replace her.

Long mustard yellow scarf

Outstretched hands during levitation

Warm woolen underskirt

FINAL FIGHT
The Ancient One's weapons of choice are magical war fans. She conjures them to battle Kaecilius and his zealots in the Mirror Dimension, though he defeats her there.

The Ancient One refuses to give the Time Stone to Bruce Banner until he reveals that Doctor Strange willingly gave it away. She trusts Stephen's plan.

WONG

Sorcerer Supreme

Master Wong is the strict librarian of Kamar-Taj. Wong is unsuccessful in his defense of the Hong Kong Sanctum against renegade mystic Kaecilius, but he stands with Doctor Strange against the evil Dormammu. Having survived the Blip, Wong helps teleport the Avengers and their allies to the battlefield where their combined forces defeat Thanos. Wong later becomes the Sorcerer Supreme.

Intense focus before casting magic spell

DATA FILE

AFFILIATION: Avengers, Masters of the Mystic Arts, Kamar-Taj, Madisynn
KEY STRENGTHS: Casting spells, encyclopedic knowledge of Mystic Arts, loyalty
APPEARANCES: DS, A:IW, A:E, SCATLOTTR, DSITMOM, SH:AAL

AMERICA'S PROTECTOR

When a giant monster starts rampaging in New York City, Wong is there in an instant, thanks to his Sling Ring. The Sorcerer Supreme teams up with Doctor Strange to protect a mysterious girl named America Chavez.

Hands poised to conjure mystical shields

Wong climbs the steep mountainside of Wundagore with the aid of a mystical rope. He's determined to stop The Scarlet Witch in the tomb of Chthon above.

Well-used sling rings

Heavy garments protect against extreme cold

SACRED TEXTS

As librarian, Wong helps Doctor Strange select reading material. Wong remarks that no knowledge is off-limits ... just certain magical practices. Doctor Strange's studies progress quickly, however, as he borrows books without Wong's permission.

MORDO
Disenchanted sorcerer

Mordo came to Kamar-Taj seeking knowledge and power. Instead, the teachings of the Ancient One brought him balance and peace. When he learns that the Ancient One has been drawing her own power from the Dark Dimension, he becomes disheartened and leaves the order, resolving to rid the world of sorcerers.

Staff of the Living Tribunal

Hand always ready to fight or cast spells

DATA FILE

AFFILIATION: Masters of the Mystic Arts, Doctor Strange, the Ancient One
KEY STRENGTHS: Casting spells, martial arts skills
APPEARANCES: DS

HELPING HAND
Mordo observes Dr. Stephen Strange searching the streets of Kathmandu for the fabled Kamar-Taj. He intervenes when robbers trap Stephen. After a scuffle, Mordo takes the desperate doctor to the Ancient One.

Elaborate handcrafted yak leather belt

Layered wool cloak

Mordo tries unsuccessfully to teach Stephen how to open a portal with a sling ring.

Vaulting Boots of Valtorr

NO OTHER WAY
When Doctor Strange expresses remorse over taking the life of one of Kaecilius's followers, Mordo calls him a coward and a whiner. Mordo tells him that they should strike their enemies first without mercy and without hesitation. He believes it's the only way to fight.

KAECILIUS
Disciple of Dormammu

Mourning the loss of his family, Kaecilius comes to Kamar-Taj to find peace. He studies the Mystic Arts under the Ancient One, covertly looking for the power to bring his family back. When he learns his teacher is secretly drawing power from the forbidden Dark Dimension, he rebels and joins the destructive Dormammu.

DATA FILE
AFFILIATION: Dormammu, Zealots
KEY STRENGTHS: Casting spells, power of the Dark Dimension
APPEARANCES: DS

Menacing stare

BLIND AMBITION

Kaecilius and his followers perform a ritual to contact Dormammu and draw power from the Dark Dimension. He doesn't realize that the eternity promised by Dormammu is, in reality, endless torment.

Kaecilius battles Doctor Strange in the Mirror Dimension, where his own powers are greatly amplified.

Warm wool leggings

SORCERER'S FOLLY

Kaecilius steals forbidden knowledge from the Book of Cagliostro. He reads only the pages with spells, failing to heed the warnings. Though he does open a portal for Dormammu, Kaecilius is imprisoned in the Dark Dimension.

Concealed inner pockets to hide stolen relics

Boot covers protect from rain

DORMAMMU

Dreadful destroyer

The extra-dimensional being known as Dormammu is a destroyer of worlds. He is at home in the Dark Dimension and seeks to devour all other dimensions in the Multiverse. Dormammu's power is seemingly infinite. When he invades Earth, aided by his disciple, Kaecilius, Doctor Strange mounts a defense and eventually forces him to retreat.

DORMAMMU'S DOOM

Dormammu uses Kaecilius to enable him to enter the world. He begins to swallow up the city and the very fabric of reality itself.

Dormammu agrees to leave and never return—taking Kaecilius and his remaining followers with him to suffer eternal torment.

Eyes emanate life force energy

DATA FILE

AFFILIATION: Dark Dimension, Kaecilius
KEY STRENGTHS: Power to consume entire dimensions
APPEARANCES: DS

TIME'S UP

Time does not exist in the Dark Dimension, which leaves Dormammu with no defense against Doctor Strange's clever strategy. Strange uses the mystical device known as the Eye of Agamotto to trap Dormammu in a time loop.

GROOT

I am Groot!

Young Groot is grown from the hero who sacrificed himself to save his fellow Guardians. This adorable Groot grows quickly into a rebellious youth. His focus turns solely to his game pad, purchased for him at a spaceport—something Rocket soon regrets. But, as the years pass, Groot becomes a young adult as steadfast and stouthearted as his predecessor.

Moss grows on top of head

Groot goes with Thor and Rocket to Nidavellir in search of a new weapon for Thor. He grabs the hot metal and forms the handle of Stormbreaker from his arm—at great pain to himself.

PINT-SIZE PLANT

The twig Rocket salvages sprouts into a new baby. He uproots himself from his pot and becomes a lovable but pesky member of the Guardians crew. Groot loves music and dancing, even during a battle.

Thick bark plates protect entire body

DATA FILE

AFFILIATION: Rocket, Guardians of the Galaxy, Thor, Knowhere
KEY STRENGTHS: Rapid growth (healing and regeneration), physical strength, durability, extendable arms
APPEARANCES: GOTG, GOTGV2, A:IW, A:E, T:LAT, GOTGV3

BUDDING HERO

With Rocket's guidance, Groot matures into a selfless hero. He's a vital part of Peter Quill's plan for the face-off inside the High Evolutionary's ship. Groot and Peter take out the armed guards surrounding them, before escaping with information they need to save Rocket.

EGO

Living planet

Ego is a Celestial, one of the oldest beings in the universe. His origins are mysterious, beginning as a brainlike being floating in space. Over eons, he formed a planet around himself and created bodies to visit other worlds. Disappointed with the life he encountered, he began a personal mission to expand his existence throughout the galaxy. He has created many children, although his Earth son, Peter Quill, is particularly unique.

DATA FILE

AFFILIATION: Mantis, Peter Quill, Meredith Quill
KEY STRENGTHS: Power to evolve, rebuild himself, and spread to other worlds
APPEARANCES: GOTGV2

CONFIDENCE GAME

Ego pretends to be a loving father to gain Peter's confidence, but his intentions are wholly evil. He only needs his son to amplify his power, much like a spare battery.

Leather belt and holster

Ornately carved silver bracers

Knee-high boots

Noble-looking robe

EXPANSION

Ego's human form can sustain itself only for a short time when it travels away from his planet. So he plants extensions of himself on worlds across the galaxy, to create permanent outposts to which he can further expand his mind.

Ego forms a planet around his core. It takes on his personality and face, which is visible from space.

MANTIS

Empathetic explorer

Mantis is a naïve and kindly insectoid who befriends the Guardians of the Galaxy when they visit Ego's world. Mantis is the daughter of Ego and half sister of Peter Quill. She is able to sense others' feelings and uses her mental powers to help Ego sleep but later turns against his evil plans. She can also use her powers to influence emotions like love, and can even completely change her target's sense of self. Mantis can hold her own in a fight.

Empathetic powers make antennae glow

DATA FILE

AFFILIATION: Ego, Guardians of the Galaxy, Knowhere, Abilisks
KEY STRENGTHS: Ability to feel what others feel, ability to induce strong emotions or deep sleep in others through touch
APPEARANCES: GOTGV2, A:IW, A:E, T:LAT, GOTGV3

NEW GUARDIAN

Mantis becomes a valuable member of the Guardians crew. She wields her powers not only to subdue Ego but also to briefly interrupt Thanos in his effort to seize the Time Stone from Doctor Strange.

Petal-like openings in sleeves

Empathetic powers activated through touch

Coattails resemble wings

MAKING FRIENDS

Drax doesn't sleep well because of the terrible loss of his family. He's excited about Mantis's ability to induce slumber—and instantly falls into a deep sleep. They become unlikely friends.

Mantis realizes the monstrous Abilisks on the High Evolutionary's ship are simply frightened and she befriends them. Later, the Abilisks are her only companions as she leaves Knowhere on a voyage of self-exploration.

MARTINEX

Pirate first mate

Martinex is the first mate of a Ravager pirate clan run by the legendary pirate, Stakar Ogord. Martinex has been a member of the crew for a long time. The original crew also included Aleta Ogord, Charlie-27, Krugarr, Mainframe, and Yondu Udonta. After Yondu's banishment, the crew disbanded, but Martinex remained as Stakar's first mate.

Cold, hard stare matches steely resolve

JUST LIKE THE OLD DAYS

Martinex pays his respects at Yondu's funeral, along with the other Ravager clans. The unexpected reunion inspires Stakar and Martinex to reassemble their old pirate crew.

Insulated jacket maintains low body temperature

SOLID AS A ROCK

Martinex's growling voice and hard, crystalline body make him seem tough as nails, but he's actually a bit of a softie on the inside. He welcomes Gamora home from a dangerous mission with a big smile.

Weapons satchel strap

DATA FILE

AFFILIATION: Ravagers, Stakar Ogord
KEY STRENGTHS: Long life span, expert thief, loyalty, resilience
APPEARANCES: GOTGV2

TASERFACE

Ravager mutineer

Taserface is a member of Yondu's Ravager crew. He tries hard—much too hard—to seem cool. He thinks Yondu has grown soft, so he revolts and imprisons his captain. Taserface shoves everyone who supports Yondu out the airlock, apart from Kraglin, Rocket, and Groot, which proves to be a fatal mistake.

Untidy mohawk

SEEDS OF REBELLION

After seeing Yondu belittled, Taserface grows unimpressed with his captain. He begins planning a mutiny with his fellow Ravagers.

DATA FILE

AFFILIATION: Ravagers
KEY STRENGTHS: Strong influencer among Ravager crew
APPEARANCES: GOTGV2

Hair braid runs along beard edge

Corroded harness buckle

The Ravagers hunt down Rocket for their Sovereign employers, but when Yondu refuses to hand him over, Taserface revolts.

RIDICULED

Taserface is not especially smart and nobody takes him seriously. Before his ship explodes, Taserface tries to exact revenge by relaying Yondu's coordinates to the Sovereign. But his contact there just laughs hysterically at his name!

Taserface's trusty blaster

AYESHA

High Priestess

The Sovereign people are renowned for their snobbish sense of superiority. Their High Priestess, Ayesha, represents them, but her interests are entirely selfish. She hires the Guardians of the Galaxy to stop the Abilisk monster, but when Rocket steals valuable Anulax batteries, Ayesha is determined to eliminate them for insulting her.

THE RISE OF ADAM
The Sovereign are genetically engineered in birthing pods. As her ultimate creation, Ayesha designs Adam with the sole purpose of destroying the Guardians of the Galaxy.

DATA FILE
AFFILIATION: The Sovereign, the High Evolutionary, Adam Warlock
KEY STRENGTHS: Sovereign military resources and funding, determination
APPEARANCES: GOTGV2, GOTGV3

Crown fused to Sovereign throne

Regal collar

Ornate golden halterneck bodice

DEVOTED MOTHER
Adam makes a lot of mistakes, but Ayesha loves him. She defends him in front of the ruthless High Evolutionary despite the risk to herself. Ayesha searches for Rocket to win favor for her and her son.

The Sovereign have thousands of remote-controlled Omnicraft, and Ayesha loses them all chasing the Guardians.

Relaxed posture conveys supreme confidence

ABILISK

Hungry monster

The Guardians of the Galaxy are hired by the Sovereign people to exterminate the terrifying Abilisk. The tentacled inter-dimensional beast is a hungry hatchling who likes to feast on the Sovereign's valuable power sources. The Guardians are given custody of Gamora's sister, Nebula, as payment for completing the task.

DATA FILE

AFFILIATION: The Sovereign, Mantis
KEY STRENGTHS: Powerful tentacles, lots of teeth, thick skin, blasts from mouth
APPEARANCES: GOTGV2, GOTGV3

Multiple rows of vicious teeth

ABILISK'S END

The Guardians look like they may lose this fight. Their weapons seem useless, until Gamora spots a wound and targets the area with her sword.

Flailing tentacles for propulsion

Hide grows thicker with age

UNEXPECTED ALLIES

Nebula, Drax, and Mantis encounter three snarling Abilisks on the High Evolutionary's ship. Mantis befriends them, realizing that the large creatures are simply scared. They go with Mantis on her new journey of self-discovery.

Having no success defeating the Abilisk, Drax leaps into its mouth, passing through rows of sharp teeth.

SCRAPPER
Scavengers of Sakaar

Castaway inhabitants of the planet Sakaar are known as Scrappers. Most, but not all, are humanoid. At first, Sakaar's ruler, the Grandmaster, liked to name them, but he quickly ran out of ideas and began assigning numbers. Scrappers scrounge the garbage heaps of Sakaar for recyclables, food, and valuable goods they can sell.

DATA FILE

AFFILIATION: Grandmaster, Valkyrie, Sakaar
KEY STRENGTHS: Resourceful, resilient, persistent
APPEARANCES: T:R

Clan mask

SCRAPPER STYLE
Scrappers wear colorful costumes made from salvaged materials. An endless rain of garbage falls from the sky to the surface of Sakaar, which makes those materials easily available to everyone on the littered planet.

SORTING TIME
When Thor crash-lands on Sakaar, he is immediately captured by Scrappers. Lately, new arrivals fall into two categories: fighters who can be sold to the Grandmaster as gladiators ... and edibles.

Loose-fitting crimson material

VALKYRIE

King of Asgard

BOUNTY HUNTER

On the planet Sakaar, Valkyrie is known as Scrapper #142. She captures new arrivals on Sakaar, like Thor, and sells them to the Grandmaster for his Contest of Champions. The Grandmaster considers her "the best."

Dragonfang sword

Valkyrie was once a member of Asgard's elite women warriors known as the Valkyrie. When the wrathful Hela wipes them all out, only Valkyrie survives. Valkyrie runs away to Sakaar, trying to forget her past. Thor convinces her to return and help him defeat Hela, although they cannot save Asgard. During the Blip, she helps establish New Asgard on Earth. Valkyrie flies into battle against Thanos on her winged horse and is later pronounced King of New Asgard by Thor.

Ragged Valkyrie cape

Valkyrie is happy to go with Thor and The Mighty Thor to Omnipotence City to find allies. She loves being King but has missed the thrill of battle.

Gilded leather belt

SPORTING SPECTATOR

Seated on her ship *Warsong* hovering above the arena, Valkyrie watches the fight between Thor and Hulk. She shows interest—momentarily—when Thor looks like he might win the contest.

One of two deadly knives

DATA FILE

AFFILIATION: The Valkyrie, Grandmaster, Asgard, Thor, Hulk, New Asgard, The Mighty Thor
KEY STRENGTHS: Strength, long life, agility, speed, combat skills, leadership
APPEARANCES: T:R, A:E, T:LAT

HELA

Goddess of Death

Hela is Odin's oldest child. Once the Executioner of Asgard, Hela led Odin's army in his conquest of the Nine Realms. Though Odin turned to peace, Hela's evil ambition was unstoppable. She rebelled and Odin was forced to imprison his daughter.

Headdress changes shape at will

Dramatic dark cloak

Outfit magically repairs itself

CLAIMING THE THRONE

When Hela returns to Asgard, she is upset that no one remembers her. Asgard's elite warriors, the Einherjar, try to stop her, but Hela single-handedly wipes out the entire army.

DATA FILE

AFFILIATION: Asgard
KEY STRENGTHS: Near invincibility, magical weapons, strength, speed
APPEARANCES: T:R

Hela tried to escape prison before. She killed almost all of Asgard's Valkyrie in the attempt.

DEADLY POWERS

Hela can magically summon an unlimited number of weapons, conjuring swords, axes, and spikes from thin air. She has an insatiable desire for power and no remorse for the immense destruction she causes.

SKURGE

Disillusioned destroyer

Skurge is an Asgardian warrior who fought alongside Thor against the invading Marauders. Skurge is later assigned to guard the Bifrost when Heimdall is banished from Asgard by Loki, disguised as Odin. Skurge is a born survivor, switching loyalties from Odin to Hela to save himself when she invades.

Lethal axe was created by Hela

MISUNDERSTOOD

Skurge may appear to be a traitor at times, but his main motivation is just to survive. He carries out Hela's bidding because, otherwise, she would destroy him, but when battle breaks out, he tries to avoid hurting others.

Sigil decorated with blue gems

FINAL DISOBEDIENCE

Hela recruits Skurge to be her Executioner, but Skurge becomes appalled by her cruelty. When it matters most, Skurge disobeys his mistress, giving his life to save the people of Asgard.

Skurge serves as Bifrost guardian but uses the opportunity to plunder the Nine Realms for souvenirs.

Armored boots are jointed to allow for movement

DATA FILE

AFFILIATION: Asgard, Bifrost, Hela
KEY STRENGTHS: Strength, adaptability, skilled combatant
APPEARANCES: T:R

THE GRANDMASTER

Game maker

Daily changing hairstyle to suit his mood

Creative and devious mind

The Grandmaster rules over the planet Sakaar and is the creator of a deadly gladiator tournament called the Contest of Champions. He is one of the oldest beings in the universe and the brother of the powerful and mysterious Collector. He leads a luxurious and indulgent lifestyle from inside his palace tower at the city center.

MASTER OF CEREMONIES

The Grandmaster's Contest of Champions pits the greatest warriors of Sakaar against each other to entertain the people. The Grandmaster promises the winner their freedom, though his latest champion, Hulk, is happy to stay.

Luxurious gold weave robe

THE CONTEST OF CHAMPIONS

The Grandmaster and Loki watch the battle between Thor and Hulk. The Grandmaster doesn't want Thor to win and gain his freedom. So he cheats and stuns Thor with his "obedience disk."

Shimmering silver lounge pants

DATA FILE

AFFILIATION: Sakaar, Topaz, The Collector
KEY STRENGTHS: Long life, manipulation, charisma
APPEARANCES: T:R

Blue toenail polish matches fingernails and chin stripe

With his loyal lieutenant, Topaz, ready and willing to use her lethal melt stick, the Grandmaster explains the Contest rules to Thor and Loki.

TOPAZ

Fierce fixer

MERCILESS
Topaz lacks empathy for those she considers beneath her. Topaz's dismissive nature makes her an enemy to anyone she finds irritating, especially Valkyrie.

Watchful gaze

Topaz is the Grandmaster's second-in-command and chief of the Sakaaran Guard. She has many roles, including the Grandmaster's personal bodyguard, food tester, accountant, head of planetary security and the air force, and the Grandmaster's all-purpose "fixer." Topaz is nearly always at the Grandmaster's side ... except when everyone revolts against him and he is overthrown.

Custom-tailored armor

HASTY SOLUTIONS
Topaz keeps an eye on Sakaar's citizens. She's quick to hand the Grandmaster his melt stick any time someone refuses to fall in line.

DATA FILE
AFFILIATION: Grandmaster
KEY STRENGTHS: Ace pilot, nasty weapons, strength of the Sakaaran Guard
APPEARANCES: T:R

Topaz pursues Valkyrie and her friends, but her ship crashes—thanks to Bruce Banner.

KORG

Stone gladiator

Body composed of perishable rock

A BIT CRUMBLY

Korg is a rocklike Kronan. After Zeus reduces his body to rubble with the Thunderbolt, only his face remains intact. But Korg is okay and in time his body regrows.

Korg is a prisoner on the planet Sakaar, where he is a gladiator in the Contest of Champions. When Thor is brought in as a new gladiator, Korg befriends him. Korg loyally stays at the God of Thunder's side from that point on—from playing video games together and adventures with the Guardians of the Galaxy to a dangerous quest to stop Gorr, the God Butcher.

WELCOMING THOR

Korg shows Thor around the gladiator stable. Korg once tried starting a revolution but failed. As punishment, he was condemned to be a gladiator.

Korg and Miek are friends. After their escape, they help fight Hela's forces on Asgard. Korg accidentally steps on Miek, but she survives.

Leather tasset protects thighs

Powerful fists

DATA FILE

AFFILIATION: Sakaar, Contest of Champions, Thor, Miek, New Asgard
KEY STRENGTHS: Strength, likability, skilled combatant, loyalty, good listener
APPEARANCES: T:R, A:E, T:LAT

MIEK

Indomitable ally

Miek is a gladiator on Sakaar when she meets Thor. Her segmented purple body fits snugly inside an advanced metal exoskeleton with long blades for hands. Without her exoskeleton, Miek is so small that her friend Korg can easily carry her under one arm when she is accidentally injured.

Entire body located at top of exoskeleton

Ambidextrous

SURVIVOR

Miek makes it through Sakaar's Contest of Champions, Ragnarok, being stepped on by Korg, the Blip, and the Battle of Earth in one piece. She's very tough, but when Thor yells at her for taking notes while he talks, it hurts her feelings.

Expertly tied bow

Hands of exoskeleton can be fitted with weapons or tools

Very squeaky whiteboard marker

Fashionable suit for the office

After the Blip, Miek moves to New Asgard with Thor and Korg. They spend their days eating pizza and playing video games. She later fights alongside the other heroes in the final battle against Thanos.

KING'S SECRETARY

Miek gets a new job in New Asgard, replacing her knives for hands with writing equipment. Miek is King Valkyrie's right-hand insectoid, from attending the opening of tourist attraction Infinity Conez to taking notes during important meetings.

Flexible joints for mobility in combat

DATA FILE

AFFILIATION: Korg, Thor, New Asgard, Sakaar
KEY STRENGTHS: Close combat, bladed weapons, battle exoskeleton, note-taking
APPEARANCES: T:R, A:E, T:LAT

FENRIS

Undead wolf

Hela rides a ferocious War Wolf named Fenris during her conquest of the Nine Realms. Though fallen in battle, Hela brings Fenris back from the dead using Odin's Eternal Flame. Fenris menaces Asgard until a struggle with the Hulk sends him falling from the brink of Asgard, just before Ragnarok begins.

DATA FILE

AFFILIATION: Hela, Asgard
KEY STRENGTHS: Strength, speed, nearly invincible, rapid healing, powerful jaws
APPEARANCES: T:R

Penetrating eyes see body heat

Coarse, matted hair

Powerful, fast-moving legs

ANIMAL INTELLIGENCE

Fenris is highly intelligent. Under Hela's orders, he tries to keep the Asgardians from escaping over the Bifrost. He would have succeeded, if not for Hulk.

DEADLY DOG

Fenris is a fearsome beast. His eyes glow like fire and his skin is bulletproof. His teeth are like knives—and one of the few things that manage to puncture Hulk's tough skin.

OKOYE
Wakandan warrior

Leadership tattoo

When she learns T'Challa survived the challenge ceremony, Okoye turns against Erik Killmonger to defend the true king.

Gold armor denotes high rank

Okoye is the personal bodyguard of King T'Challa and the fierce leader of the royal guard known as the Dora Milaje. She is also a personal friend and trusted advisor to the king. Okoye accompanies T'Challa on missions to other countries and defends Wakanda against the forces of Thanos. When she's stripped of her rank as general, she protects her country with fellow guard Aneka, in a team named the Midnight Angels.

DATA FILE

AFFILIATION: Wakanda, Dora Milaje, T'Challa, Midnight Angels

KEY STRENGTHS: Dora Milaje training, speed, agility, hand-to-hand combat with spear; with Midnight Angel armor: flight, superhuman strength and durability

APPEARANCES: BP, A:IW, A:E, BP:WF

Traditional Dora Milaje vibranium spear

DUTY FIRST

After Erik Killmonger takes over, Nakia urges Okoye to flee with her, Ramonda, and Shuri. However, Okoye stays behind to defend the throne, no matter who sits on it.

LOYALTY

Okoye swore an oath to protect the king. When her husband W'Kabi betrays T'Challa, she stands against him. Okoye's loyalty to Wakanda always comes first and she defends her beloved country whether she's the general of the Dora Milaje or a civilian.

PRINCESS SHURI

Black Panther

Shuri is a brilliant inventor and Princess of Wakanda. The scientific genius develops new vibranium technology, including advanced medical devices, remote-controlled flying ships, and powerful weapons. Shuri helps her brother, T'Challa, win back the throne of Wakanda from Erik Killmonger and plays a crucial role in the battle against Thanos. After the Blip, Shuri loses T'Challa to illness, and she feels at fault for not finding a cure in time.

Helmet and suit are of Shuri's design

STAND FIRM

Shuri stands with her brother against the usurper Killmonger. Her vibranium gauntlets are strong, but their blasts are absorbed by Killmonger's suit.

Shuri attempts to safely disconnect the Infinity Stone in Vision's forehead before Thanos finds him.

Hidden ship controls

Retractable vibranium claws

PAINFUL PATH

Shuri has an independent mind and a strong will. She seeks revenge against Namor, the ruler of Talokan, for the death of her mother. But Shuri overcomes her need for vengeance, and the two kingdoms ultimately reach a peaceful agreement.

DATA FILE

AFFILIATION:
Wakanda, T'Challa, Queen Ramonda

KEY STRENGTHS:
Scientific genius, intelligence, innovation, creativity; as Black Panther: enhanced strength, speed, and agility, vibranium armor and claws

APPEARANCES: BP, A:IW, A:E, BP:WF

Shuri recreates and consumes the Heart-Shaped Herb that grants the Black Panther their abilities. She becomes Wakanda's new protector.

ERIK KILLMONGER

Righteous rival

Erik Stevens, a.k.a. N'Jadaka, is the son of N'Jobu, the brother of Wakanda's former king, T'Chaka. When N'Jobu attacked Zuri, a friend of the royal family, T'Chaka killed him. Young Erik was abandoned in Oakland, California, where he devoted his life to taking revenge on the Wakandan royal family. He later takes the throne of Wakanda, declaring himself king.

Royal ring of grandfather King Azzuri

Killmonger uses a vibranium artifact at the Museum of Great Britain to gain the confidence of the criminal Ulysses Klaue.

Fragmentation grenade

DATA FILE

AFFILIATION: Former member of Wakandan royal family
KEY STRENGTHS: Navy SEALs and Black Ops training, power of the Black Panther, conviction in his belief to change Wakanda
APPEARANCES: BP, BP:WF

Camouflage cargo pants

DEALER OF DEATH

Killmonger earns his menacing nickname because of his many victories. He deliberately seeks out the most dangerous missions to prepare himself for mortal combat against T'Challa.

KING NO MORE

Just when Killmonger thinks he is secure as Wakanda's new king, T'Challa returns. Killmonger dons an advanced Black Panther suit of his own and attacks.

QUEEN RAMONDA

Majestic matriarch

Ramonda, daughter of Lumumba, is the mother of T'Challa and Shuri and the widow of King T'Chaka. She sits on the council of elders where she helps govern Wakanda. After King T'Challa's tragic death, Queen Ramonda takes the throne as sovereign ruler. She rules fairly but firmly. She isn't intimidated by other nations' attempts to steal Wakandan resources or by Namor's threats.

ON THE RUN

When Erik Killmonger seizes power after defeating T'Challa in ritual combat, Ramonda and Shuri flee for their lives. They meet Nakia and Everett Ross before looking to the Jabari Tribe for help.

Kimoyo Beads

SACRIFICE

Ramonda bears the heartbreaking losses of her husband and her son for the good of Wakanda. But when her daughter, Shuri, is kidnapped while under General Okoye's protection, her overwhelming grief can't be held back any longer.

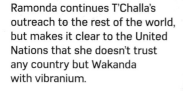

WAKANDA

Ramonda continues T'Challa's outreach to the rest of the world, but makes it clear to the United Nations that she doesn't trust any country but Wakanda with vibranium.

Regal silk gown

DATA FILE

AFFILIATION: Wakanda, T'Chaka, T'Challa, Shuri
KEY STRENGTHS: Complete dedication to family, duty to country, resilience
APPEARANCES: BP, BP:WF

NAKIA
Solitary spy

Nakia is a respected member of the River Tribe and the War Dogs, Wakanda's intelligence agency. The brave and resourceful spy goes on undercover missions to Nigeria and across Africa, as well as overseas to countries like South Korea. Her work brings her closer to King T'Challa, and in time they act on their undeniable feelings for each other.

ABSENCE
After T'Challa's passing, Nakia takes time for herself to heal. She returns to duty when Queen Ramonda personally asks her to rescue Shuri from Namor's underwater kingdom. Nakia succeeds, and she stays at the royal family's side until the Talokan threat is resolved.

Lightweight armor for quick movement underwater

FIERCE FIGHTER

Nakia is a skilled fighter and trained in martial arts. Always putting her country first, she wears the armor of the Dora Milaje, Wakanda's royal guard, when helping T'Challa fight Erik Killmonger and the Border Tribe.

Kimoyo Beads for communication

Nakia and Okoye chase smuggler Ulysses Klaue through the busy streets of Busan, South Korea.

Vibranium circular blade

DATA FILE

AFFILIATION: Wakanda, River Tribe, War Dogs, T'Challa, Wakandan royal family
KEY STRENGTHS: War Dog training, espionage, fighting skills, intelligence, fluency in multiple languages
APPEARANCES: BP, BP:WF

Insulation in suit retains body heat

Nakia is thrilled when T'Challa agrees to open Wakanda to aid people from other countries.

AYO
Head of security

Ayo is the right hand of General Okoye and serves as the Dora Milaje Security Chief for King T'Challa of Wakanda. She stays close to the king on his travels. When the Winter Soldier, Bucky Barnes, comes to Wakanda to heal, Ayo supports him through his rehabilitation. Later, Ayo bravely defends Wakanda in the battle against Thanos's forces.

Vibranium spear

Red Dora Milaje uniform

DATA FILE
AFFILIATION: Wakanda, Dora Milaje, T'Challa, Aneka, Bucky Barnes
KEY STRENGTHS: Dora Milaje combat training, speed, agility
APPEARANCES: CA:CW, BP, A:IW, TFATWS, BP:WF

TIME'S UP
Ayo and the Dora Milaje arrive to take Zemo back into custody after Bucky Barnes breaks him out of prison. She takes down Captain America John Walker without breaking a sweat and disables Bucky's metal arm with just a touch.

Hand-tooled vibranium bracers

KING AND COUNTRY
As a member of the Dora Milaje, Ayo must watch T'Challa's challenge ceremony without interfering. When Erik Killmonger is victorious, Wakandan law says she must protect him as king.

Ayo becomes General and commands the Dora Milaje after Okoye is stripped of her rank. She later leads the charge against Namor's forces on the deck of the *Sea Leopard*.

W'KABI

Border Tribe leader

DATA FILE

AFFILIATION: Border Tribe, Wakanda, T'Challa, Okoye, Erik Killmonger
KEY STRENGTHS: Skilled fighter, controls Border Tribe army
APPEARANCES: BP

W'Kabi's tribe lives in Wakanda's highlands where they raise livestock. W'Kabi is King T'Challa's best friend, but he loses faith in him when T'Challa fails to apprehend Ulysses Klaue, the man responsible for W'Kabi's father's death. When Erik Killmonger gets the job done, W'Kabi sides with him against T'Challa.

RHINO RIDER

W'Kabi raises battle rhinos and summons them when T'Challa challenges Killmonger. The beasts charge through the Dora Milaje like battering rams, but unfortunately for W'Kabi, the rhinos love his wife, Okoye, who stops them in their tracks.

Patterned blue and silver cloak

CHANGE OF HEART

The Border Tribe is defeated by the Dora Milaje and W'Kabi surrenders when Okoye confronts him. Though W'Kabi is a traitor, his tribe later helps the Black Panther fight Thanos's forces.

When W'Kabi allies himself with Killmonger against the true king T'Challa, it drives a wedge between him and Okoye.

ULYSSES KLAUE

Dangerous weapons dealer

Ulysses Klaue is a South African arms dealer and criminal. He worked with Prince N'Jobu to steal a fortune in vibranium from Wakanda. Klaue sold his share to Ultron but lost his arm when Ultron lost his temper. He acquires a replacement prosthetic arm fitted with a vibranium sonic cannon. Klaue is betrayed by N'Jobu's son, Erik Killmonger, when they team up to steal more vibranium.

Claw necklace over tattoo

CIA agent Everett K. Ross tries to lure Klaue into a trap at the Busan Casino, but the villain spies T'Challa and escapes.

CRIMINAL RECORD

Klaue is a wanted man for crimes against Wakanda. He has already been caught stealing vibranium once, for which he was branded on his neck. Klaue is also responsible for the death of W'Kabi's parents in an explosion he caused at the Wakandan border.

Chamber conceals vibranium cannon

Cybernetic hand

Mix tape in pocket

THREATENING FOE

The Black Panther, Okoye, and Nakia track down Klaue in Busan, South Korea, hoping to bring him to justice. Klaue uses the deadly sonic cannon concealed inside his synthetic arm to attack his pursuers.

DATA FILE

AFFILIATION: Erik Killmonger, Ultron
KEY STRENGTHS: Cybernetic arm, underworld contacts
APPEARANCES: A:AOU, BP

M'BAKU

Jabari Tribe leader

The Jabari Tribe live in the snowy highland peaks of Wakanda. M'Baku is the leader. His people shun the use of vibranium technology. M'Baku resents Wakanda's ruling family but makes peace and comes to T'Challa's aid when Erik Killmonger threatens their nation's future, and again when Thanos invades.

DATA FILE

AFFILIATION: Jabari Tribe, Wakanda
KEY STRENGTHS: Hand-to-hand combat, physical strength, Jabari army, wisdom
APPEARANCES: BP, A:IW, A:E, BP:WF

OPPONENT

M'Baku challenges T'Challa for the throne. Wearing a wooden mask, M'Baku fights fiercely at the challenge ceremony. He fails, however, and leaves in peace.

Studded panels over fur gauntlets

Club-staff weapon

GIVING

M'Baku is generous and cares deeply for his country. He promises T'Challa he will offer advice and protection to Shuri. After Namor's attack on the capital, he agrees for people evacuated from the city to come to Jabariland.

Knee-cap protector

M'Baku is uneasy about the consequences of the conflict between Wakanda and Talokan. He questions Shuri whether killing Namor and risking eternal war is the right action.

ZURI

Spiritual leader

Zuri is the high priest of Wakanda and a close friend to both T'Chaka and his son, T'Challa. In his youth, Zuri was sent on an undercover mission for King T'Chaka to spy on his brother, Prince N'Jobu. During a confrontation, T'Chaka killed N'Jobu to save Zuri. Years later, Zuri is murdered by N'Jobu's son, Erik Killmonger, after offering himself for T'Challa's life.

Tabard decorated with beads, wood, and bones

A TERRIBLE SECRET

Zuri feels guilty for betraying T'Chaka's brother N'Jobu and abandoning his son N'Jadaka (Killmonger) in America. After T'Challa sees Killmonger's royal ring, Zuri finally confesses the truth.

DATA FILE

AFFILIATION: Wakanda, T'Chaka, T'Challa
KEY STRENGTHS: Loyalty to the royal family, self-sacrifice, knowledge of Wakandan lore
APPEARANCES: BP

Long purple robe

KEEPER OF THE HEART-SHAPED HERB

As a spiritual advisor and friend to the royal family, Zuri is trusted with many secrets. Among them is tending the cave of Heart-Shaped Herbs that bestow the power of the Black Panther.

Zuri oversees the challenge ceremony. He strips Prince T'Challa of the Heart-Shaped Herb's power before the fight.

EITRI

Mighty blacksmith

Eitri is a master weapons forger and one of the Dwarves of Nidavellir. He is entrusted by Odin with creating the magical weapons of Asgard, including Thor's hammer, Mjolnir. After Mjolnir is destroyed, Eitri helps Thor create a new hammer called Stormbreaker, believed capable of destroying Thanos.

DATA FILE

AFFILIATION: Dwarves of Nidavellir, Thor, Asgard

KEY STRENGTHS: Can create the universe's most powerful weapons

APPEARANCES: A:IW

Sturdy harness strap

SEARCH FOR THE MASTER

Eitri's reputation for his craft is known across the universe. After Thor's hammer is destroyed, he seeks Eitri out. Eitri does not recognize the God of Thunder at first.

Fireproof clothing

SAD END

Thanos forces Eitri to craft the Infinity Gauntlet for him. When finished, Thanos wipes out all Eitri's people and encases Eitri's hands in metal to prevent him from crafting any more weapons.

When Thanos leaves Nidavellir, it is desolate. The forge is off and the dying star is dark.

Metal-covered hands

EBONY MAW

Voice of Thanos

Ebony Maw is one of Thanos's adopted children. Gifted with the power of eloquent speech, he is also known as "The Maw." Maw speaks on Thanos's behalf when he destroys Gamora's homeworld. Maw is also tasked with recovering the Time Stone, but he gets sucked into space along the way. A past version of Maw from 2014 fights in the Battle of Earth and is defeated again.

Sparse white hair

MIND OVER MATTER

Maw is neither physically imposing nor in possession of a weapon. He doesn't need any because his powerful mind is capable of controlling the environment around him through telekinesis.

TIME STONE QUEST

Ebony Maw restrains Doctor Strange aboard his ship. He hopes to force Doctor Strange to hand over the Time Stone before they reach Thanos on his homeworld, Titan.

Armored tunic

Hands direct telekinetic powers

DATA FILE
AFFILIATION: Thanos
KEY STRENGTHS: Telekinesis, levitation, skilled manipulator
APPEARANCES: A:IW

CORVUS GLAIVE

Deadly tactician

Corvus Glaive is one of Thanos's adopted children. Glaive helps Thanos conquer worlds and acquire the powerful Infinity Stones. His mission on Earth is to recover the Mind Stone from the Avenger Vision, but Glaive is injured in Scotland and later perishes in Wakanda. A version of Glaive from the past expresses concern for Thanos's troops in the Battle of Earth, where he ultimately meets his end again.

Hood shields skin from light

Elflike earpiece

Glaive's weapon is so resilient it can deflect energy beams fired by the Mind Stone without taking damage.

SHARP-EDGED

Glaive wields a powerful bladed staff that pierces Vision's body and prevents him from phase-shifting. He almost pries the Mind Stone from Vision's head with the curved blade before Wanda intervenes. Later, Vision uses Glaive's own weapon against him in a fatal strike.

FIERCE FOE

Corvus Glaive is a powerful fighter. On his quest to obtain the Space Stone for Thanos, he boarded an Asgardian ship and took down most of the crew himself.

Cowl with gold detailing

Flexible body armor

DATA FILE

AFFILIATION: Thanos
KEY STRENGTHS: Strength, speed, durability, extraordinary weapon
APPEARANCES: A:IW

PROXIMA MIDNIGHT

The Spear of Thanos

Proxima Midnight is sent by her "father," Thanos, to recover the Mind Stone. She and her partner, Corvus Glaive, stalk Vision and Wanda Maximoff from Europe to Africa. Proxima leads Thanos's Outrider army against Wakanda, but meets her end on the battlefield. A past version of Proxima from 2014 fights in the Battle of Earth but disappears with the rest of Thanos's forces.

Horns grow from temples

WEAPONS MASTER

Proxima Midnight is skilled in hand-to-hand combat. Her preferred weapon is a three-pronged spear that fires bolts of energy. She also wields a sword and blades in her wrist gauntlets.

Heavy armor on arms for close combat

OUTNUMBERED

Proxima and Corvus Glaive corner Vision and Wanda Maximoff at a train station in Edinburgh, Scotland. Fortunately, Steve Rogers intervenes, forcing the villains to flee.

In Wakanda, Proxima attacks Wanda Maximoff, but Okoye and Black Widow come to Wanda's aid.

Stretch armor glove

Double-edged sword

DATA FILE

AFFILIATION: Thanos
KEY STRENGTHS: Strength, agility, speed, hand-to-hand combat
APPEARANCES: A:IW

CULL OBSIDIAN

Brute of Thanos

One of the children of Thanos, Cull Obsidian is large and terrifying. The beast gets his name from how effective he is at brutally reducing populations who have been conquered by Thanos. Cull joins the hunt for Earth's two Infinity Stones, but he is beaten by Bruce Banner in the battle in Wakanda. A past version of Cull joins Thanos's army in the Battle of Earth—until the giant Ant-Man squashes him.

PULLED AWAY

Cull Obsidian battles Tony Stark in New York City, allowing Ebony Maw to retrieve the Time Stone from Doctor Strange.

UNUSUAL WEAPON

Cull Obsidian's unique weapon has many functions. It can fire a projectile on a chain and transform into a shield.

Skull protected by natural armor

Bandolier holds spare hammer blades

DATA FILE

AFFILIATION: Thanos
KEY STRENGTHS: Strength, durability, cybernetic arm, unusual weaponry
APPEARANCES: A:IW

Shapeshifting weapon

Hand later replaced with prosthetic

Powerful legs

AVA STARR

Ghost

Ava Starr is the daughter of former S.H.I.E.L.D. agent Elihas Starr. Her father steals quantum technology from Dr. Hank Pym and conducts tests that accidentally kill him and his wife in an explosion. Ava survives, but her body is transformed, allowing her to shift between quantum dimensions and pass through objects.

FAILING SUIT

S.H.I.E.L.D. trains Ava Starr as an assassin, and Dr. Bill Foster creates a suit to help control her painful phase-shifting. However, it proves insufficient, so she plans to drain healing quantum energy from Janet Van Dyne.

Mask distorts voice

Suit swipe controls

Suit designed to help manage pain and phase-shifting

Ghost uses her athletic skills to steal a motorcycle and chase the van carrying Hank's miniaturized lab.

DESPERATE MEASURES

Ava begins the process to extract quantum energy from Janet and use it to heal her own molecular structure. She watches in wonder as her hand starts to seem more solid.

DATA FILE

AFFILIATION: Dr. Bill Foster, S.H.I.E.L.D.
KEY STRENGTHS: Quantum phase-shifting (invisibility and passing through objects)
APPEARANCES: AMATW

DR. BILL FOSTER

Rogue scientist

Dr. Bill Foster is a former S.H.I.E.L.D. agent. He worked with Dr. Hank Pym on Project Goliath, where they experimented with Pym Particles to expand body mass. Bill achieved a height of 21 ft (6.4 m) but left S.H.I.E.L.D after a falling out with Hank. The determined scientist secretly mentored a troubled young S.H.I.E.L.D. agent, Ava Starr (code name: Ghost), promising to cure her harmful quantum phase-shifting.

QUANTUM SCIENTIST

Bill left S.H.I.E.L.D. before the rise of Hydra and became a professor. He teaches cutting-edge theoretical science.

Casual jacket

DATA FILE

AFFILIATION: S.H.I.E.L.D., Dr. Hank Pym, Ava Starr
KEY STRENGTHS: Scientific expertise, compassion
APPEARANCES: AMATW

Bill works in a lab at Ava's hidden lair, trying to counteract the effects of her condition.

FOSTER'S GHOST

Bill and Ava have developed something of a father-daughter relationship over the years. Bill will do everything in his power to ease Ava's pain and save her life.

JIMMY WOO

FBI agent

Jimmy Woo is an FBI agent. He serves as Scott Lang's law enforcement custodian after Scott violates the Sokovia Accords. Jimmy is also on the lookout for Dr. Hank Pym and Hope Van Dyne, who originally provided Scott with the Ant-Man suit he wore while helping Captain America. Later, when Jimmy can't get in touch with a witness, he travels to Westview, New Jersey, to find them.

Freshly pressed regulation FBI suit

MISSING TOWN

Jimmy is one of the first to notice something is very wrong in Westview. He works with S.W.O.R.D. agent Monica Rambeau and Dr. Darcy Lewis to get to the bottom of the mystery.

HOUSE SEARCHES

It is Jimmy Woo's job to make sure that ex-con Scott Lang stays at home and doesn't violate his house arrest. Scott does leave the house, but Jimmy is never able to catch him.

Polished FBI badge worn with pride

DATA FILE

AFFILIATION: FBI, Scott Lang, Dr. Darcy Lewis, Monica Rambeau
KEY STRENGTHS: FBI resources, dedication, integrity, sleight of hand
APPEARANCES: AMATW, WV, AMATW:Q

SONNY BURCH

High-tech smuggler

Shady gangster Sonny Burch has access to rare technology needed by Hope Van Dyne to finish building the Quantum Tunnel. Hope tries to buy the component from Sonny, but he takes her money and refuses to hand it over. The stand-off leads to a fierce and ongoing struggle between Sonny and The Wasp.

Slick manner masks a menacing streak

Garish, flashy tie

DESPERATE MEASURES
With the FBI after them, Hope Van Dyne and her father must deal with smugglers like Sonny Burch to get the tech needed to build the Quantum Tunnel and find her mother.

BAD BUSINESS
Sonny's untrustworthy practices make him an unreliable associate at best, and treacherous at worst. Most people do business with him only once.

Sonny will do whatever it takes to get his hands on Dr. Pym's miniaturized lab. He's not interested in the Quantum Realm. He simply wants to sell off the technology inside.

DATA FILE
AFFILIATION: Criminal underworld
KEY STRENGTHS: Criminal market connections, gang resources, spies inside the FBI
APPEARANCES: AMATW

CAROL DANVERS

Captain Marvel

Kree soldier Vers finds herself on planet Earth, where she is tracked down by S.H.I.E.L.D. agent Nick Fury. They eventually join forces to help the shapeshifting aliens called Skrulls, and Vers regains her memories of her life as Carol Danvers. Later, as Captain Marvel, she travels the universe using her powers to protect other planets. Captain Marvel returns to Earth when Thanos's use of the Infinity Stones prompts Fury to call her for help.

STARFORCE
As "Vers," Carol is a part of the elite Kree military unit Starforce. She discovers that the Kree were manipulating her and containing her powers. She breaks free of their control and embraces her unlocked abilities, which include flight and survival in space. At her full strength, Captain Marvel is almost invulnerable.

Repurposed symbol of Starforce

Uniform colors chosen by Monica Rambeau

Cosmic energy focused in hands

PILOT PAST
Carol Danvers eventually remembers her past, in which she was a U.S. Air Force pilot. She was a top pilot, with fast reflexes and exceptional courage.

DATA FILE
AFFILIATION: Starforce, Kree Empire, Nick Fury, Maria Rambeau, Monica Rambeau
KEY STRENGTHS: Superior piloting abilities, enhanced durability, strength and reflexes, cosmic energy blasts, healing abilities, space flight
APPEARANCES: CM, A:E, MM, TM

At the Battle of Earth, Captain Marvel destroys Thanos's command ship singlehandedly. As she trades punches with Thanos, he recognizes her strength.

SUPREME INTELLIGENCE

Cunning mind

The Supreme Intelligence is an A.I. that rules the Kree civilization from the capital of Hala. It has presided over generations of Kree, but no one knows what the true form of the Supreme Intelligence looks like. Its appearance is chosen by the mind of the individual speaking to it.

Cold expression

Leather flight jacket

INFINITE SPACE

The Supreme Intelligence exists in a limitless area that it can shape by will. Liquid metal communication devices are required to establish a link to it and enter its space.

Project Pegasus patch

Hands in pockets in imitation of Mar-Vell

BLANK SLATE

The Supreme Intelligence materializes as someone the beholder deeply admires. Vers sees it as a human woman, although she has no memory of who the woman is or why she is important to Vers.

The Supreme Intelligence may be highly intelligent, but it's also manipulative and cunning. It lies about the danger of the Skrulls to cling to power—and uses Carol's abilities for its own benefit.

DATA FILE

AFFILIATION: Kree Empire
KEY STRENGTHS: Strategy, analysis, self-preservation
APPEARANCES: CM

YON-ROGG
Kree commander

Yon-Rogg is the commander of Starforce, a squad of combat specialists in the Kree army. He leads the team with confidence and the rousing battle cry, "For the good of all Kree!" Vers serves under his command on Starforce until she remembers her past as Carol Danvers. She realizes that Yon-Rogg took advantage of her memory loss to control her to fight on the Kree's side.

Combat helmet

Helmet provides enhanced vision for detecting threats

FOR ALL KREE
As part of the Kree military forces, Yon-Rogg is completely loyal to the Supreme Intelligence and the empire. He has no sympathy for the Skrulls and will do whatever it takes to win their interplanetary war.

Starforce uniform

Team symbol

Bracer emits energy shield

SIDE BY SIDE
Vers and Yon-Rogg are more than just teammates. Vers received a transfusion of Yon-Rogg's blood before she first awoke on the planet Hala. They're genuinely friends—but Yon-Rogg's duty to the Kree always comes first.

Armor protects from energy blasts

Standard issue Kree boots

Yon-Rogg sees himself as a mentor to Vers and acts as her sparring partner and advisor. He encourages her to strictly control her emotions so she can be a better warrior.

DATA FILE
AFFILIATION: Starforce, Kree, Supreme Intelligence, Vers
KEY STRENGTHS: Military and combat training, gravity gauntlets, strategy and tactics, manipulation
APPEARANCES: CM

MAR-VELL

Selfless scientist

Mar-Vell is a Kree scientist who doesn't agree with the unjust war against the Skrulls. She offers the fleeing Skrulls safety on her hidden ship. Afterward, she focuses on developing light-speed engine technology to help the Skrulls get far away from the Kree once and for all. Mar-Vell continues her research on Earth, where she poses as Dr. Wendy Lawson. Maria Rambeau and Carol Danvers become her test pilots—and friends.

THE TESSERACT
Mar-Vell obtains a mysterious energy core from S.H.I.E.L.D. to power her light-speed engine. She calls it the "Tesseract." The Space Infinity Stone—which will later play a vital role in the universe's future—is inside.

Project Pegasus patch

Mar-Vell accompanies Carol on a test flight. She isn't developing the cosmic energy-powered spacecraft to fight wars, but to end the conflict.

Fitted leather bomber jacket

SACRIFICE
Starforce tracks Mar-Vell to Earth and brings down her experimental spacecraft, the *Asis*. After it crashes, the injured scientist tells Carol the truth about who she really is. Mar-Vell tries to destroy the spacecraft's engine before the Kree find it, but she fails.

DATA FILE
AFFILIATION: Project Pegasus, Carol Danvers, Maria Rambeau, Skrulls, Kree
KEY STRENGTHS: Brilliant scientist and inventor, Kree technology, the Tesseract
APPEARANCES: CM

MARIA RAMBEAU

Founder of S.W.O.R.D.

When Carol Danvers and Nick Fury arrive at her Louisiana home, Maria Rambeau is amazed. She and Carol were once close. Six years earlier they worked as test pilots for the *Asis*, an experimental plane developed by Dr. Wendy Lawson. When it was destroyed, Maria took the apparent loss of Carol hard.

Pilot name badge

Air Force base patch

FOUNDER

After Carol departs from Earth, Maria establishes the Sentient Weapon Observation Response Division, also known as S.W.O.R.D. The purpose of this government agency is to monitor space for possible threats.

MARIA "PHOTON" RAMBEAU

FIGHTER AND PILOT

Maria wants to make a difference as a pilot, even though women are not allowed to fly combat for the Air Force. She and Carol work on Project Pegasus, testing aerospace technology.

Fitted helmet protects head during high-speed acceleration

Flame-resistant flight suit

DATA FILE

AFFILIATION: Monica Ramheau, Carol Danvers, U.S. Air Force, S.W.O.R.D.
KEY STRENGTHS: Skilled fighter pilot, Air Force combat training
APPEARANCES: CM, WV

Carol, Maria, and her daughter Monica were as close as a real family. The two women worked and played hard together, too.

GOOSE
Friendly Flerken

Carol Danvers and Nick Fury investigate the well-guarded site of Project Pegasus. In the halls of the military facility, they meet Dr. Wendy Lawson's affectionate tabby cat. The name tag on her collar reads "Goose." Goose is a sweet kitty, but there's more to her than meets the eye.

DATA FILE

AFFILIATION: Captain Marvel, Nick Fury, Mar-Vell

KEY STRENGTHS: Extendable tentacles, razor-sharp claws, high perception

APPEARANCES: CM, TM

Sensitive whiskers detect vibrations in air

STOWAWAY

When Carol and Fury make a quick getaway from the facility, they jump on board an aircraft. They hear meowing as the ship blasts off and discover Goose came along for the ride. She stays by Fury's side.

COOL CAT

Talos is alarmed when he sees Goose inside Maria Rambeau's house, and Starforce considers the Flerken species very dangerous—all for good reason. Goose uses her powerful tentacles to swallow hostile Kree soldiers whole.

Silver name tag

Orange tabby markings

Goose is an alien species known as Flerken. She has powerful tentacles and can safely store dangerous items like the Tesseract inside her body.

BRON-CHAR
Starforce heavyweight

Every member of the Starforce squad has their own specialty. The bruiser Bron-Char is the muscle. But he's never eager to pick a fight. Bron-Char keeps a cool head under pressure during a search and rescue mission to find a missing spy on the planet Torfa. He waits for orders before responding to the local population's threatening presence.

Cranium ridges

CAMARADERIE
Bron-Char and the other members of Starforce fight together like a well-oiled machine. They need to work on their banter, however. Bron-Char responds to Vers's good-natured teasing with a sincere compliment for his teammate Korath.

DATA FILE
AFFILIATION: Starforce, Kree
KEY STRENGTHS: Strength, durability, military training in combat and weapons
APPEARANCES: CM

Well-groomed beard

Starforce members attempt to take the Tesseract from Captain Marvel. Bron-Char gives it everything he's got, from exchanging energy-boosted blows to swinging an entire pinball machine at her. However, the squad is soundly defeated.

Starforce team uniform

TRUE WARRIOR
Bron-Char is an expertly trained fighter who knows how to use his large size and colossal strength to his advantage. Bron-Char throws powerful jabs with the added force from the energy fields his weapons generate around his hands.

MINN-ERVA

Serious sharpshooter

Minn-Erva is a valuable member of Starforce and repeatedly saves the elite team from sticky situations. The Kree sharpshooter has keen eyes and years of training with long-range weapons. A high-tech mask and cutting-edge scope aid Minn-Erva when scouring through dusty air for her target.

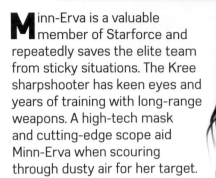

Tactical sniper veil

Bandolier stores long-range ammunition

STRAIGHT SHOOTER

The Kree sniper is direct and honest. When Captain Marvel asks why they never hang out, Minn-Erva answers plainly that she doesn't like her.

DUTY

Under Yon-Rogg's command, Minn-Erva follows orders without question. She holds her fire as ordered after Carol Danvers destroys the experimental starship drive they were searching for.

Starforce team uniform

DATA FILE

AFFILIATION: Kree, Starforce
KEY STRENGTHS: Long-range weapons expert, sharpshooting, piloting, quick thinking
APPEARANCES: CM

Minn-Erva is a capable pilot, but she struggles to keep up with ace fighter pilot Maria Rambeau in a high-speed chase.

Reinforced suit protects joints and vital areas

TALOS

Skrull spy

Talos is the leader of a group of Skrull aliens fighting against the Kree through deception and espionage. The Skrulls have waged a fierce battle against the alien Kree Empire for centuries, leading to the destruction of Skrullos. Talos's desperate search for refugees—including his wife, Soren, and daughter, G'iah—brings him to Earth, where he meets S.H.I.E.L.D. agent Nick Fury. An unlikely friendship begins.

Pointed ears are an identifying Skrull trait

Reptilian skin is the natural Skrull form

Suit changes with body when shapeshifting occurs

SHAPESHIFTER

Skrulls are known for shapeshifting, which they call "simming." They can impersonate anyone they see, which enables them to blend in for intelligence gathering and sabotage. Talos is particularly skilled at simming.

PLANET C-53

Talos and his agents capture Vers because she shares the same energy signature as Mar-Vell's experimental engine. Talos searches her memory for clues. Vers's connection to Planet C-53, Earth, is their best lead for finding the Kree scientist's hidden ship. The Skrulls quietly arrive on the unsuspecting planet.

Talos poses as Nick Fury's superior, Keller, to keep track of Vers. He slips up by addressing Nick as Nicholas.

DATA FILE

AFFILIATION: Skrulls, Soren, G'iah, Nick Fury
KEY STRENGTHS: Shapeshifting ability, intelligence, military strategy, espionage
APPEARANCES: CM

CAPTAIN MONICA RAMBEAU

Rising star

Monica Rambeau follows in her mom's footsteps by joining S.W.O.R.D. (the Sentient Weapon Observation and Response Division.) As a child, Monica knew Captain Marvel and is rarely shocked when she sees something out of the ordinary. However, her encounter with Wanda Maximoff's reality-altering energy changes Monica inside and out.

S.W.O.R.D. ID badge

STRANGE FORCE FIELD

Monica is tasked by S.W.O.R.D. with a new assignment. She takes an imaging drone to investigate a missing persons case in Westview, New Jersey. She's suddenly pulled inside the town and becomes Geraldine, Wanda's friend and neighbor.

LIGHT SOURCE

Walking through Wanda's magical Hex gives Monica the ability to see and manipulate energy along the electromagnetic spectrum. She can also change her physical form to absorb energy and become intangible.

Despite the danger to herself, Monica pushes through the Hex to get back into Westview after Wanda forces her out. Monica is determined to bring Dr. Darcy Lewis to safety.

DATA FILE

AFFILIATION: Maria Rambeau, Captain Marvel, S.W.O.R.D., Nick Fury, Kamala Khan, Jimmy Woo, Dr. Darcy Lewis

KEY STRENGTHS: Bravery, persistence, S.A.B.E.R. astronaut training, ability to see the light spectrum, energy absorption, intangibility, flight

APPEARANCES: CM, WV, TM

S.W.O.R.D.-issued tactical pants

2014 THANOS

Inevitable villain

When Nebula travels back in time to 2014 to retrieve the Space Stone from Morag, she inadvertently alerts the Nebula and Thanos of the past. Thanos learns that he succeeds in the future. He and 2014 Nebula devise a plan to bring his ship and army to the future, where he can obtain all six Infinity Stones at once.

Helmet protects head from lethal strikes

DIFFERENT APPROACH

Thanos realizes that there will always be resistance to his plan if there are people who remember how things were before. He decides to destroy this universe and create a new one instead.

ANNOYING LITTLE PLANET

Thanos conquers countless planets and eliminates lives, but insists it's never out of personal spite or hatred. Earth's stubborn heroes, however, annoy him. He tells the Avengers that he will enjoy destroying their planet.

Nebula's memory file gives Thanos a glimpse at the future, including his own death. He accepts his fate as his destiny fulfilled.

Double-bladed sword capable of slicing vibranium

DATA FILE

AFFILIATION: 2014 Nebula, Ebony Maw, Corvus Glaive, Chitauri
KEY STRENGTHS: Overwhelming strength, stamina, and durability, loyal army, conviction
APPEARANCES: A:E

Armor withstands most physical and energy attacks

2014 NEBULA

Loyal look-alike

The Nebula of 2014 is dedicated to serving her father, Thanos, and finding the Infinity Stones. When her future self is revealed to be an ally of the Avengers, Nebula desperately declares her loyalty to the Titan. She proves it when she takes the place of the future Nebula, hacks the Avengers' time machine, and brings Thanos and his ship, the *Sanctuary II*, into the future.

DUTIFUL DAUGHTER

Nebula isn't interested in Thanos's plan for cosmic balance. She seeks only her father's approval and will do whatever it takes to make him proud. Not even a future version of herself can convince Nebula to leave Thanos and his villainy behind.

WRONG SIDE

In 2014, Nebula still sees her sister, Gamora, as competition for their father's attention. She bitterly refuses Gamora's helping hand and ultimately chooses Thanos over Gamora. 2014 Nebula remains loyal to him, even when given the chance to change, and she loses her life as a result.

Clothing for utility, not comfort

Internal cybernetic enhancements

DATA FILE

AFFILIATION: 2014 Thanos, 2014 Gamora
KEY STRENGTHS: Enhanced strength, durability, and self-repair; cyborg components interact with technology
APPEARANCES: A:E

2014 Nebula removes the future Nebula's metal headpiece. She wears it as a disguise to impersonate her future self and enters the Avengers Compound unsuspected.

Energy pistol

2014 GAMORA

Ruthless Ravager

DATA FILE

AFFILIATION: Ravagers, Nebula, Guardians of the Galaxy, 2014 Nebula

KEY STRENGTHS: Highly trained assassin and fighter, martial arts, speed, agility, strength

APPEARANCES: A:E, GOTGV3

The Gamora of 2014 is on board Thanos's ship when it's brought to the present as the Battle of Earth begins. This Gamora hasn't met Peter Quill and the Guardians of the Galaxy yet, and she's not that impressed when she does. She is close to her sister, Nebula, however, and answers her call when the Guardians need help accessing data to save Rocket's life.

Cybernetically enhanced reflexes

Holster belt secures sword for quick access

Collapsible blade

EARLY DAYS

Before the Guardians of the Galaxy exist, Gamora already has doubts about Thanos's quest for the Infinity Stones. She also hopes for a closer relationship with Nebula. Nebula of the present welcomes 2014 Gamora as a sister, although the two take different paths.

RAVAGER

Instead of tagging along with the Guardians, 2014 Gamora joins the ranks of the Ravagers as a mercenary for hire. She has no affection for any of the Guardians except Nebula.

Quill tells 2014 Gamora that he and the other version of her were in love. Gamora is unconvinced and mistakenly calls him "Quinn."

LOKI (TVA)

Time traveler

In one diverging timeline, Loki seizes the opportunity to escape from New York with the Tesseract. The Time Variance Authority (TVA), overseen by the Time Keepers, sends its hunters to retrieve him and states that he is a variant, number L1130. Loki quickly finds out there's more to the TVA than meets the eye. His quest to discover the true nature of the Time Keepers shakes the entire Multiverse to its core.

TOGETHER

Loki feels an immediate connection with Sylvie, another variant. Together, they make it through imprisonment by the TVA and more than one world-ending apocalypse. Loki stays by her side as they confront the person who's controlling the Time Keepers—and time itself.

Well-pressed pants

Hair flipped back

GLORIOUS PURPOSE

The TVA has hunted many Loki variants and no two are exactly the same. One dangerous Loki variant is particularly hard to find, so TVA agent Mobius offers Loki the chance to help. In return, he might be given a chance to speak to the Time Keepers.

Patch bearing the TVA motto, "For all time, always"

Standard-issue TVA necktie

Loki stands trial for his crime against the Sacred Timeline. Judge Renslayer isn't swayed by his argument that the Avengers are at fault for altering the timeline. She finds Loki guilty.

DATA FILE

AFFILIATION: Time Variance Authority, Sylvie, Mobius
KEY STRENGTHS: Illusion magic, long life, rapid regeneration, deception, TVA devices for time travel
APPEARANCES: A:E, L

AGATHA HARKNESS
Power-hungry witch

Agatha Harkness has been practicing spellcasting for hundreds of years. Sensing Wanda Maximoff's magic in Westview, she is intrigued by the number of complicated spells cast simultaneously on the town and its residents. Agatha realizes that Wanda is capable of reality-altering Chaos Magic. She decides that dangerous power should be in her own hands.

Agatha plays the role of the nosy neighbor to perfection. She pretends to be a friend of the Maximoffs while waiting for Wanda to show her true self.

Mark of the Darkhold, a magic book

Flowing robe

WITCH'S TRIAL

As a young witch in Salem, Massachusetts, Agatha was punished by her coven for studying dark magic. While under attack, she absorbed the power of the other witches and turned it against them to save herself—an ability she didn't know she had. Her mother—her main accuser—was among the fallen.

Cameo once belonged to her mother

DATA FILE

AFFILIATION: Salem coven, Darkhold
KEY STRENGTHS: Spellcasting, absorbing magic power of others, runes, mind control, illusion
APPEARANCES: WV

AGATHA ALL ALONG

Agatha sends Westview resident Ralph Bohner to Wanda's doorstep, posing as her brother, to add to the tension in her ideal family life. Agatha's meddling purposely puts stress on Wanda's spells to nudge her awake from her fantasy.

WESTVIEW VISION

Dream husband

Keeps up with fashions of the 1950s

Genuine smile for his neighbors

Vision is a loving husband and father who lives in Westview, New Jersey. He and his wife, Wanda, are the picture of married bliss. He's a friendly neighbor and a hardworking employee. But Vision can't shake the feeling that not everything in their small town is as it seems …

NEW LIFE
Vision has no memory of his life before Westview. As he puts the pieces of his past together, he realizes that while he might not be real because he is a creation of Wanda's Chaos Magic, his love for his family is.

Wears a suit to the office every day

MODEL CITIZEN
Vision stops by the local neighborhood watch meeting at the Westview library. He pretends to be human so that he and Wanda can fit in with the people in their town.

Westview Vision matches wits and fists with White Vision. They conclude that they are both Vision and both not Vision. They are each something new.

DATA FILE

AFFILIATION: Wanda Maximoff, Vision, Billy Maximoff, Tommy Maximoff
KEY STRENGTHS: Artificial intelligence, intangibility, flight, illusion, family
APPEARANCES: WV

WHITE VISION
Rebuilt and repurposed

The government agency S.W.O.R.D. retrieved Vision's body after the Snap. They dismantled the remains and rebuilt his vibranium body to a new one they could control. The result was White Vision, who lacks the original's consciousness and memories. His mission? To destroy Westview Vision.

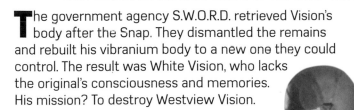

Energy beam no longer powered by Mind Stone

White Vision and Westview Vision take to the skies in a battle among the clouds. Westview Vision asks if they can resolve things peacefully, but White Vision declares his opponent must be destroyed.

Carbon-based synthezoid

HEARTLESS

White Vision has the data of the original Vision's memories but cannot access them. He has no affection for Wanda and attacks her without emotion. She's too shocked to stop him, but Westview Vision arrives just in time to save her.

Cape and other components from original Vision

Systems jumpstarted by Wanda's magic

DATA FILE

AFFILIATION: S.W.O.R.D., Vision

KEY STRENGTHS: Artificial intelligence, intangibility, flight, energy beam

APPEARANCES: WV

I AM VISION

Westview Vision unlocks the memories and experiences being kept from White Vision. The restored synthezoid immediately leaves Westview of his own free will. His whereabouts are unknown.

BILLY MAXIMOFF

Telepathic twin

Billy Maximoff is born in Westview to Wanda Maximoff and Vision. He quickly grows up through the lens of a television sitcom, getting into one wild situation after another. Billy is part of the altered reality that Wanda's Chaos Magic unintentionally creates. The Maximoffs might be an unconventional family, but their bond is strong.

Telepathic connection to Vision

Favorite T-shirt

DORKASAURUS REX

Billy is the more cautious and contemplative of the twins. He's also awkward and known to trip on his own feet. Tommy dubs Billy a Dorkasaurus Rex, but with affection. The brothers love each other dearly.

LIKE MOM, LIKE SON

Billy's super-powers appear on Halloween night when he senses Vision is in danger. Like Wanda, Billy's mental abilities include telepathy and telekinesis. He stops a bullet in midair when a S.W.O.R.D. team opens fire in the middle of Westview.

Outstretched hand focuses telekinesis

Billy and his brother, Tommy, have fun celebrating Halloween. Later, they both disappear when the Westview illusion ends. Wanda becomes determined to find them in a universe where they can all be together.

DATA FILE

AFFILIATION: Wanda Maximoff, Vision, Tommy Maximoff, Westview
KEY STRENGTHS: Telepathy, telekinesis, loving family
APPEARANCES: WV

TOMMY MAXIMOFF

Speedy sibling

Tommy Maximoff, son of Wanda Maximoff and Vision, is Billy's twin brother. He grows up quickly in Westview—and discovers he can move quickly, too, when his super-speed manifests on Halloween night. Like Billy and the Vision in this illusion, Tommy is created from the Chaos Magic that Wanda Maximoff wields.

Hat and sunglasses stolen from S.W.O.R.D. agents

The Maximoff family is surrounded by a menacing synthezoid, a 300-year-old witch, and armed soldiers, but they make a stand and face them together.

Comfy T-shirt

FAMILY IS FOREVER

Tommy and Billy feel the tension between their parents as Vision searches for the truth about Westview. Wanda reassures the boys that their family will always love one another.

New appreciation for tracksuits

DATA FILE

AFFILIATION: Wanda Maximoff, Vision, Billy Maximoff, Westview
KEY STRENGTHS: Super-speed and stamina, loving family
APPEARANCES: WV

THE "COOL" ONE

Tommy is more laid-back and carefree than Billy, and thinks he is the cooler of the Maximoff twins. Egged on by his uncle Pietro, Tommy skips trick-or-treating. Instead, he uses his newfound powers to prank the neighborhood at super-speed.

RALPH BOHNER

Bogus brother

Wanda Maximoff is stunned when she sees Pietro Maximoff, her brother lost in Sokovia years earlier, standing in her doorway. He doesn't look the same, but he claims to be the same Pietro. In reality, he's Ralph Bohner, a Westview resident. Ralph is a run-of-the-mill slacker until Agatha Harkness's mind-control magic involves him in Wanda's life.

Windswept hair from super-speed

Wanda and Vision welcome Pietro into their home and treat him like part of the family—but he's not who he says he is. He's been sent by Agatha to gain information about Wanda's powers.

Necklace is source of Agatha's mind-control spell

LONG LOST

Wanda doesn't understand how Pietro has been resurrected or why he looks different. He still acts like a brother, however, and lends Wanda a sympathetic ear when she needs one.

HELD HOSTAGE

Agatha takes Ralph's home as her own while she keeps an eye on Wanda. He's sent to a room upstairs to live, where he spends his days watching old movies and playing guitar until Agatha has a use for him.

Scrounged Halloween costume

DATA FILE

AFFILIATION: Westview, Wanda Maximoff, Agatha Harkness
KEY STRENGTHS: Super-speed
APPEARANCES: WV

JOAQUIN TORRES

Inside man

First Lieutenant Joaquin Torres is an easygoing intelligence officer in the U.S. Air Force. Joaquin is assigned to assist Sam Wilson, AKA Falcon, during an unofficial mission to save a kidnapped military captain. He provides Sam with the real-time updates that he needs for a successful rescue. Joaquin cheers enthusiastically as Sam returns with the captain.

DATA FILE

AFFILIATION: U.S. Air Force, Sam Wilson
KEY STRENGTHS: Military and combat training, reconnaissance, intelligence gathering
APPEARANCES: TFATWS

WINGMAN

Joaquin helps Sam with intel on the Flag Smashers, even though the pair are not officially working together. After the wings of the Falcon suit are ripped off, they meet to discuss next steps. Sam tells Joaquin to keep the broken pieces.

Friendly grin

Off-duty casual clothes

CHATTER

Joaquin and Sam have lunch in a Tunisian café after the mission. Joaquin tells Sam about the Flag Smashers, a troubling group he's tracking online as a potential concern. They believe the world was better during the Blip. Joaquin assures Sam that it wasn't.

Joaquin watches as Sam, the new Captain America, gives a speech from the heart about doing the right thing even when it's not easy. He nods in agreement.

KARLI MORGENTHAU

Flag Smasher

At first, Karli Morgenthau just wants to help similar displaced people like her, who lost their homes or jobs after the end of the Blip. Karli creates the Flag Smashers, an underground activist group who believes in a world without borders. As they become increasingly violent to accomplish that goal, she gets the attention of Sam Wilson, the Falcon.

Sam, now Captain America, tries to reason with Karli instead of fighting. But he has to intervene when she points a gun at Sharon Carter.

Well-worn jacket

ONE WORLD, ONE PEOPLE

The Flag Smashers fight the efforts of the Global Repatriation Council to deport refugees, who lost their homes when the original residents returned from the Blip. Karli and her group see themselves as freedom fighters. They're quietly supported by people around the world.

BETRAYAL

Although Karli initially worked with The Power Broker, aka Sharon Carter, she steals The Power Broker's Super Soldier Serum and leaves to form the Flag Smashers.

DATA FILE

AFFILIATION: Flag Smashers, Power Broker
KEY STRENGTHS: Activism, leadership, hand-to-hand combat; with Super Soldier Serum: enhanced strength, agility, stamina, and durability
APPEARANCES: TFATWS

Ripped combat pants

JOHN WALKER

Captain America / U.S.Agent

Highly decorated U.S. Army officer John Walker is selected by the government to become the next Captain America. He meets Sam Wilson and Bucky Barnes after their first conflict with the Flag Smashers, but they don't give him a warm welcome. John uses all his resources to search for the group's leader. But as the losses pile up, he begins to buckle under the pressure of being Captain America. When John finds an unbroken vial of the Flag Smashers' Super Soldier Serum, he can't resist the temptation to use the serum himself.

SECOND CHANCE
Contessa Valentina Allegra de Fontaine takes an interest in John after his military discharge. She knows the super soldier could come in handy, so she gives him a new uniform and dubs him "U.S.Agent."

Flag patch shows government affiliation

STAR-SPANGLED MAN
John knows he'll have to live up to high expectations as the new Cap. He's introduced to the world alongside marching bands, sparkly dancers, and fireworks. John signs autographs and poses for selfies, but he's eager to start the real work.

Originally Steve Rogers's shield

DATA FILE
AFFILIATION: U.S. government, Lemar Hoskins, Contessa Valentina Allegra de Fontaine
KEY STRENGTHS: Extensive military and special ops training, hostage rescue, vibranium shield; with Super Soldier Serum: enhanced agility, strength, and stamina
APPEARANCES: TFATWS

Thick leather combat boot covers

The death of his best friend Lemar Hoskins causes John to kill one of the Flag Smashers in a rage. He is stripped of his rank and is no longer Captain America.

ISAIAH BRADLEY

Hidden super soldier

During the Korean War, the U.S. military ran secret tests on Black soldiers to recreate the Super Soldier Serum used on Steve Rogers. Isaiah Bradley was the only success. He was unjustly jailed for 30 years after the war, and his blood was taken for tests without his consent. Many years later, Bucky Barnes and Sam Wilson visit Isaiah for a possible lead on new super soldiers.

FIGHT IN GOYANG

The U.S. military sent Isaiah to find the Winter Soldier, formerly Bucky, in Korea. Isaiah took on the Hydra assassin and survived, damaging the Winter Soldier's metal arm.

NEVER FORGOTTEN

The hidden history of Isaiah and the other Black soldiers in his unit stayed buried for decades—until Sam uses his connections to bring it to light. He shows Isaiah a new exhibition at a museum's Captain America memorial, which honors Isaiah and the soldiers.

Body has super soldier abilities from secret experiments

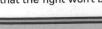

Despite his misgivings about Sam taking the name of Captain America, Isaiah knows Sam is special. Isaiah warns him that the fight won't be easy.

DATA FILE

AFFILIATION: U.S. military, Eli Bradley, Sam Wilson
KEY STRENGTHS: Military training; with Super Soldier Serum: enhanced strength, agility, and durability
APPEARANCES: TFATWS

DIRECTOR DE FONTAINE
Power player

Contessa Valentina Allegra de Fontaine, the director of the CIA, always knows more than she lets on. After the end of the Blip, she begins searching for a different kind of special individual. Whether it's the former Red Room assassin Yelena, or the former Captain America John Walker, Valentina looks beyond their past mistakes and recognizes their talents.

CIA analyst Everett Ross reports to Director de Fontaine, who is also his ex-wife. She arrests Ross for sharing intelligence with the Wakandans.

GRAY AREA

Valentina introduces herself to the disgraced John Walker after his trial. She voices her support of his actions even if others don't approve. She tells John not to worry about retrieving Cap's vibranium shield. Valentina whispers that it doesn't belong to the government anyway.

Sharp wool coat

CIA badge in pocket

DATA FILE

AFFILIATION: CIA, Everett Ross, John Walker, Yelena
KEY STRENGTHS: Espionage, intelligence gathering, manipulation
APPEARANCES: TFATWS, BP:WF

THE CONTESSA

Valentina's full name and title are Contessa Valentina Allegra de Fontaine. She tells John that she knows it's hard to say. It's okay for him to use the nickname Val—as long as he doesn't say it out loud.

MOBIUS

Astute agent

Agent Mobius is an analyst for the Time Variance Authority (TVA). Like everyone in the TVA, Mobius works to protect the proper flow of time from variants—individuals who veer off the path the Time Keepers created. He specializes in the pursuit of dangerous variants. Mobius recruits a Loki variant, L1130, to help him locate another, particularly dangerous Loki variant who has been targeting the TVA's hunters.

UNIMPRESSED

Mobius isn't intimidated by the fuming God of Mischief (aka L1130.) He's seen a lot of Lokis in his line of work, so he's not concerned about this variant's threats. Mobius asks the aggravated Asgardian some hard questions, to better understand the Loki variant he's chasing.

ANOTHER LIFE

Mobius doesn't know where he's from or anything about the life he had before he worked for the TVA. He likes to think he had a personal watercraft in those happy days.

Plain, unfashionable suit

DATA FILE

AFFILIATION: Time Variance Authority, Ravonna Renslayer, Hunter B-15, Loki variant L1130

KEY STRENGTHS: Investigation and analysis, navigating bureaucracy, fieldwork, time manipulation devices

APPEARANCES: L

Time Twister

After Mobius learns that everyone in the TVA—including himself—is a variant, he decides to help the Loki variants find answers. The Sacred Timeline completely fractures as a result.

Standard TVA necktie

RAVONNA RENSLAYER

Blindsided bureaucrat

Ravonna Renslayer works for the Time Variance Authority, first as a hunter and later as a judge. Her job is to protect the proper flow of time, called the Sacred Timeline, as dictated by the Time Keepers. When one of her favorite agents, Mobius, asks permission for a Loki variant to assist him on an investigation, Ravonna reluctantly agrees.

Neatly knotted tie

Ravonna and Mobius have been co-workers and close friends for eons. She feels betrayed when he sides with the Loki variants against the TVA. She orders the hunters to prune Mobius.

JUDGE AND JURY

As a well-respected judge of variants—individuals who disrupt the Sacred Timeline—Ravonna is unmoved by the desperate shouts and bravado of Loki variant L1130. She sentences him to be pruned from the timeline.

TempPad stores timeline data and opens Time Doors

Crisp, clean judge uniform

TVA-issue wristwatch

SEARCHING

Despite the growing evidence that the TVA isn't what she thinks it is, Ravonna believes in their mission and ideals. Her hard work couldn't have been for nothing. She leaves the TVA headquarters on a personal mission to find answers.

DATA FILE

AFFILIATION: Time Variance Authority (TVA), Time Keepers, Mobius
KEY STRENGTHS: Bureaucracy, levelheadedness, hunter combat training, time manipulation devices
APPEARANCES: L

SYLVIE

Vexing variant

A particular Loki variant evades the grasp of the Time Variance Authority. She attacks the TVA's agents, and is considered very dangerous. This enigmatic variant, whose chosen name is Sylvie, mistrusts the Loki variant L1130 when she first comes face to face with him. Initially she refuses to ally with him, but eventually Sylvie lets her guard down.

ENCHANTING
Sylvie's magic requires physical contact to influence another mind. Some minds are trickier than others. To control a strong mind, Sylvie creates a fantasy from its memories in order to hold the connection.

NO TIME TO LOSE
The TVA took Sylvie from her Asgard when she was just a young girl. She escaped and has been on the run through time ever since. Sylvie wants to put an end to the TVA so it cannot interfere with the timeline of anyone else.

Clothing inspired by her timeline's Asgardian armor

Neither wants to admit it, but Loki and Sylvie are kindred spirits. They feel an instant connection that goes beyond both of them being Loki variants.

Experienced fighter

DATA FILE
AFFILIATION: Loki
KEY STRENGTHS: Enchantment, memory retrieval, survival
APPEARANCES: L

HUNTER B-15

Serious sentry

B-15 is a Hunter in the Minutemen, the TVA's enforcers. They keep the Sacred Timeline intact by capturing variants. B-15's team tracks a rogue Loki variant to a supermarket serving as a shelter from a hurricane. B-15's mind is overtaken by the variant and her world shaken up by what she sees.

B-15 confronts Sylvie about what she saw while enchanted. It was a glimpse of B-15's life before the TVA, which she didn't know existed.

CAPTURING LOKI

In one alternate timeline, Loki uses the Tesseract to escape after the Battle of New York. Hunter B-15 finds him in Mongolia and arrests the variant for his crimes against the Sacred Timeline. She's not phased by his dismissive attitude.

Rigid chest protector

Equipment holster

Arm and shoulder guard

FOR ALL TIME

As a Hunter, B-15 is a natural leader—tough, tenacious, and no-nonsense. She has never been known to question orders ... until she meets Sylvie.

DATA FILE

AFFILIATION: Time Variance Authority (TVA), Minutemen, Mobius
KEY STRENGTHS: Leadership, hand-to-hand combat, sense of duty
APPEARANCES: L

Activated Time Stick vaporizes variants

TVA-issued tactical uniform

YELENA

Spirited assassin

Yelena was the youngest member of the pretend family put together by General Dreykov for an undercover operation. But to young Yelena, her family was real. After their successful assignment, Yelena was taken away to train as a Widow. Years later, she breaks free of the Red Room's control. She starts her own mission to free other Widows, which leads her back to her sister, Natasha Romanoff.

Tactical vest modified by Yelena

LOTS OF POCKETS

A green tactical vest is the first piece of clothing Yelena ever buys for herself. She loves that she finally has control of her own decisions—and that the vest holds a lot of objects in its handy pockets. Yelena lends it to Natasha.

CIA director Valentina Allegra de Fontaine hires Yelena to kill Clint Barton. Yelena attacks him, and she angrily confronts him about his responsibility for Natasha's death. They talk out their feelings and come to an understanding.

REUNION

Yelena and Natasha fight to a standstill the first time they reunite. Yelena sent her the antidote for the Red Room's brainwashing for the Avengers to analyze, but Natasha isn't on speaking terms with them. The explosive arrival of more Widows interrupts their catch up.

Red Room–issued tactical gloves

White suit for snow camouflage

Padding for joint protection

Military-grade combat boots

DATA FILE

AFFILIATION: Natasha Romanoff, Melina, Alexei Shostakov, Red Room
KEY STRENGTHS: Highly trained assassin, weapons handling, espionage
APPEARANCES: BW, H

ALEXEI SHOSTAKOV

Red Guardian

Alexei Shostakov is the Soviet Union's first super soldier. He operates under the name Red Guardian. Alexei works as a spy for General Dreykov, assigned to steal S.H.I.E.L.D. intel while posing as part of a normal family in Ohio. He longs to return to action in his bright red suit, but Dreykov has other plans for him.

Symbolic star

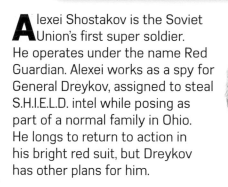

Alexei spent three years in the Ohio suburbs pretending to be Natasha and Yelena's father. He loves them like they're his own daughters. Alexei is proud of their work as successful spies and assassins.

White utility belt

ESCAPE

Widows Natasha Romanoff and Yelena need to find the Red Room, and they hope Alexei can tell them where it is. They break him out of a freezing Russian prison in a daring escape, but they don't give him a warm welcome.

Red color matches the Soviet flag

Reinforced bracers provide defense

GREAT ADVERSARIES

As a super soldier, Red Guardian has enhanced physical abilities comparable to Captain America. He considers Cap an equal and contemporary, even though they've never faced each other.

DATA FILE

AFFILIATION: USSR, Melina, Yelena, Natasha Romanoff, General Dreykov
KEY STRENGTHS: Enhanced strength, agility, and durability, training in espionage
APPEARANCES: BW

MELINA

Red Room researcher

Melina and Alexei lived a normal life in Ohio with two young girls, Natasha and Yelena. In reality, they were all Dreykov's undercover agents. The family barely escaped after S.H.I.E.L.D. uncovered their activities. Melina loved the girls, but they were sent away to train as spies. Years later, Melina is continuing her research in mind control on a remote farm when she reunites with Natasha, Yelena, and Alexei.

SCIENTIFIC MIND

Melina was the architect of Dreykov's mind control experiments. She used stolen S.H.I.E.L.D. research to develop brainwashing. This was then used to control Widows and other subjects around the world.

STRANGE LOVE

Their marriage might have been fake, but Alexei and Melina created their own version of a loving family. The spark between them is still there years later.

Neatly
braided hair

Work
clothes

DATA FILE

AFFILIATION: Red Room, Alexei Shostakov, Natasha Romanoff, Yelena
KEY STRENGTHS: Trained combatant, espionage, weapons handling, piloting, scientific experimentation
APPEARANCES: BW

Sleeves
often
covered in
mud

Melina thinks fast and doesn't get overwhelmed when things don't go her way. She does whatever it takes to get the job done.

GENERAL DREYKOV

Spy master

General Dreykov is the mastermind behind the Red Room, an ultra-secret organization of spies and assassins known as Widows. He abducts girls and begins their indoctrination and training at a very young age. Dreykov keeps his Widows firmly under his thumb by removing their free will.

Believes himself to be highly intelligent

SPY NETWORK

Dreykov believes real power isn't found in flashy Super Hero battles but in invisible influence from the shadows. Hundreds of his hidden agents are positioned around the world—ready to change the course of history at his command.

Expensive custom-made suit

INSURANCE

Dreykov uses a form of mind control to make sure none of his Widows can hurt him. Even though Natasha Romanoff escaped his clutches years ago, her own body stops her from striking him when she has the chance.

After his undercover agents complete their mission, Dreykov uses the Hydra intelligence they stole to develop mind control technology.

DATA FILE

AFFILIATION: Red Room, Taskmaster, Black Widow
KEY STRENGTHS: Espionage, assassination, intelligence gathering, brainwashing
APPEARANCES: BW

ANTONIA DREYKOV

Taskmaster

Taskmaster is the unyielding agent who General Dreykov deploys only for top-priority missions. Capable of mirroring the combat skills of opponents, Taskmaster is a challenging foe for both Natasha Romanoff and her sister Yelena. But Taskmaster isn't just a special project of Dreykov's. She is his daughter, whom Natasha believed she killed years ago.

Visor displays combat data and mission objectives

Antonia Dreykov was just a girl when Natasha Romanoff detonated an explosion in General Dreykov's office. Antonia survived but received injuries to her face and body.

Bulletproof shield with Taskmaster symbol

Helmet controls in hidden wrist panel

RELENTLESS

When the Taskmaster Protocol is activated, Antonia has no choice but to follow General Dreykov's orders. She continues to pursue Natasha even as the Red Room falls from the sky. Antonia resumes her attack after a hard landing on the ground below.

Retractable-bladed sword can be stored in armor on back

Can flawlessly duplicate Black Widow's leg grapple

PERFECT MIMIC

Taskmaster replicates the fighting styles of the Avengers and their allies, including Captain America, Hawkeye, Black Panther, and Black Widow. She gives Red Guardian the match against Captain America he's always wanted.

Concealed knife

DATA FILE

AFFILIATION: General Dreykov, Red Room
KEY STRENGTHS: Mirrors others' skills, including shield-throwing, archery, and hand-to-hand combat; suit provides tactical analysis, enhanced strength, and durability
APPEARANCES: BW

Thick-soled boots

RICK MASON
Resourceful supplier

Rick Mason is the guy who can get whatever you need. He helps Natasha Romanoff with everything from a gas-powered generator for her off-the-grid hideout to forged passports, driver's licenses, and a fully prepped helicopter. Given enough time and resources, Mason can find just about anything, including a functional Quinjet.

While Mason and Natasha have a professional partnership, he's also been a good friend to her when she needs one—whether she admits it or not.

Well-worn leather jacket

WELL-CONNECTED

Mason and Natasha obviously have a long history together. He's the one person she turns to for help when she's on the run from the government. Mason's not afraid to tease her by giving her silly false identity names, though Natasha isn't amused.

PRIVATE CONTRACTOR

The hunt for Natasha puts Mason on Secretary Ross's radar. Mason's business hInyes on secrecy and he begins to lose clients as a result. Natasha promises to make it up to him.

DATA FILE

AFFILIATION: Natasha Romanoff, Yelena
KEY STRENGTHS: Procurement, criminal market knowledge, discretion
APPEARANCES: BW

SHANG-CHI
Martial arts master

Shang-Chi leaves his old life in China behind as an assassin-in-training when he's a teenager. Shang-Chi, who now goes by Shaun, floats aimlessly through life. He works as a valet in San Francisco with his best friend Katy—until his father, Wenwu, decides it's time for Shang-Chi to come home.

GREAT PROTECTOR
The people of the hidden village of Ta Lo keep watch over the Dark Gate, which holds back the monstrous Dweller in Darkness. When it breaks through, Shang-Chi uses the mystical power of the Ten Rings to prevent it from destroying the world.

Shang-Chi started learning how to fight when he was just seven years old. He now uses his formidable martial arts abilities to save lives instead of taking them.

STARTING OVER
Shang-Chi isn't just on the run from his father. He's also trying to escape from the guilt of taking a life in revenge. He finds a new purpose as a hero after he inherits the mysterious Ten Rings—ancient rings of incredible power.

Flexible dragon-scale armor

Highly skilled in hand-to-hand combat and melee weapons

DATA FILE
AFFILIATION: Katy, Xialing, Ta Lo, The Ten Rings
KEY STRENGTHS: Speed, agility, flexibility, martial arts, parallel parking
APPEARANCES: SCATLOTTR

Reflexes honed by years of rigorous martial arts training

KATY

Brave bestie

FEELING AIMLESS

While Katy isn't unhappy as a valet, she feels she doesn't have much of a direction in life. She wishes she could find her own passion and dedication, much like the residents of Ta Lo.

Katy is a valet driver who works with her best friend Shaun. When Katy learns about Shaun's hidden past as a highly trained fighter, she drops everything to go with him to find his sister in Macau. They eventually make their way to the secret village of Ta Lo, where Katy discovers a talent for archery.

Quiver of handcrafted arrows

Dragon scale accents

Lightweight but powerful wooden bow

STEADFAST

Whether it's facing a bully in high school, saving the Earth from the Dweller in Darkness, or meeting the Sorcerer Supreme, Katy stands firmly by Shaun's side.

Dragon scale tipped arrow

DATA FILE

AFFILIATION: Shang-Chi, Xialing, Ta Lo, Guang Bo

KEY STRENGTHS: Courage, high-speed driving, archery, causing confusion

APPEARANCES: SCATLOTTR

Ta Lo archer uniform

Katy breaks the rules and takes a customer's car for a quick joyride, much to Shaun's disapproval.

WENWU

Ten Rings leader

Thousands of years ago, Wenwu gained the power of the Ten Rings, although it's unknown where he found the mysterious artifact. He used the strength and long life they granted him to build an army, called The Ten Rings. Generations passed. Wenwu remains unsatisfied, despite his power—until his search for the hidden village of Ta Lo brings him to Li, who later becomes his beloved wife.

Leather pauldrons

DATA FILE

AFFILIATION: The Ten Rings, Li, Shang-Chi, Xialing, Razor Fist
KEY STRENGTHS: Martial arts training, criminal empire, influence, wealth; with the Ten Rings: long life, enhanced strength, agility, and durability
APPEARANCES: SCATLOTTR

Flexible leather body armor

Rings glow with an otherworldly blue light

Support and protection for waist

WARLORD

Wenwu conquers every foe that stands in his way. The Ten Rings on his arms grant him astonishing powers—from defending against a barrage of arrows to taking out the enemy's front line without breaking a sweat.

UNLIKELY LOVE

Li, guardian of Ta Lo, defeats the would-be invader Wenwu in a hand-to-hand fight through her own training and the magic of the Great Protector. Wenwu and Li's delicate dance of combat draws them to each other with every graceful grapple and elegant kick.

Tactical combat boots

Wenwu never stops watching over his children Shang-Chi and Xialing, even though they both ran away from him. There is anger and resentment between the three of them, but also love.

LI

Graceful guardian

The Ten Rings' leader, Wenwu, is seeking the legendary village of Ta Lo. Standing in his way is the sentinel Li, an agile and adept martial artist. After the unlikely pair eventually falls in love, Li leaves Ta Lo and her incredible powers behind. She and Wenwu become parents to Shang-Chi and Xialing.

Traditional Ta Lo robe

NEW LIFE

Li shows Wenwu a different way of looking at the world. As a result, he gives up the Ten Rings. Li and Wenwu begin a joyful life together in China, raising their two children. However, their happy existence does not last.

No armor, for ease of movement

DATA FILE

AFFILIATION: Ta Lo, Wenwu, Shang-Chi, Xialing, Ying Nan
KEY STRENGTHS: Martial arts, wind manipulation, magic of the Great Protector
APPEARANCES: SCATLOTTR

PROTECTOR

The Iron Gang comes looking for revenge against Wenwu, but he isn't at home. Li asks the men to spare her children and then faces them alone and without fear. They leave the children but take Li's life as payback.

Li takes time to teach her children about where they come from. She hopes they will visit her beloved home one day.

XIALING

Shadowy self-starter

Shang-Chi left his younger sister, Xialing, behind when he went to America. The loss hit Xialing hard. She also left home soon after turning 16 years old but chose a different path from that of her brother. Xialing went to Macau and started building an ambitious new life her own way.

White dragon scale armor

SELF-TAUGHT

Wenwu refused to train his daughter with the boys. Xialing learned martial arts by watching from the shadows and taught herself how to do it better. The rope dart—a long rope with a metal blade on one end—is Xialing's weapon of choice.

Learned martial arts by observation

LASHING OUT

Xialing owns an underground fighting ring called the Golden Daggers Club. When Shang-Chi turns up at the club, she channels her resentment at being abandoned by stepping into the ring with him. Blood ties mean nothing to Xialing. She doesn't pull any punches.

Tunic handcrafted by Ta Lo artisans

Loose clothing for freedom of movement

The Ten Rings organization finds a smart new leader in Xialing. She won't let a prime opportunity pass her by.

Kicks are as powerful as any weapon

DATA FILE

AFFILIATION: Shang-Chi, Wenwu, Li, The Ten Rings
KEY STRENGTHS: Martial arts, rope dart mastery, entrepreneurship, natural leader
APPEARANCES: SCATLOTTR

YING NAN

Astute auntie

Ying Nan is a wise protector who calls Ta Lo home. Nan is Li's sister and the aunt of Shang-Chi and Xialing. She warmly welcomes them to the hidden village. Nan gives the siblings insight into their family's long history.

GUARDIAN

For thousands of years, the people of Ta Lo have protected all universes from the Dweller in Darkness. Nan and the other villagers guard its prison, empowered by the magic of the Great Protector.

Long, intricate braid

Simple robe worn by the keepers of the Dark Gate

Dragonfly wing pendant

GIVING GUIDANCE

Nan gracefully reminds Shang-Chi of the lessons he learned from his mother. She shows him to approach an opponent with an open hand instead of a closed fist. Nan shares her wisdom quietly, but every word she says is powerful.

When The Ten Rings arrive in Ta Lo, Nan tries to resolve matters through talking first. She appeals to Wenwu's memory of her sister, but he won't listen.

DATA FILE

AFFILIATION: Ta Lo, Li, Shang-Chi, Xialing
KEY STRENGTHS: Hand-to-hand combat, staff weapons, air manipulation, wisdom
APPEARANCES: SCATLOTTR

RAZOR FIST

Dutiful deputy

Razor Fist is one of Wenwu's most trusted lieutenants in The Ten Rings. Wenwu tasks the warrior with retrieving a valuable pendant from Shang-Chi. The Ten Rings choose a San Francisco city bus ride to stage their ambush. After his men are taken out by Shang-Chi, Razor Fist deftly wields his powerful prosthetic arm and its sizzling energy blade to launch his own forceful attacks.

DATA FILE

AFFILIATION: The Ten Rings, Wenwu
KEY STRENGTHS: Blade prosthetic on lower arm, hand-to-hand combat, leadership, loyalty
APPEARANCES: SCATLOTTR

COMBATANT

Razor Fist is skilled in close combat and the use of melee weapons. He's able to hold his own against the highly trained Shang-Chi.

The Ten Rings combat uniform

Advanced prosthetic socket easily switches weapons

Energy blade can slice through metal

Razor Fist isn't unreasonable. He agrees to a truce with Xialing and Ying Nan, and they join forces against the Dweller in Darkness.

Reinforced tactical pants

LOYAL

Razor Fist remains devoted to The Ten Rings even after Wenwu's death. He dutifully works for their new leader, his former adversary Xialing.

DEATH DEALER

Ten Rings teacher

Death Dealer is one of The Ten Rings' highest-ranking members. Wenwu chooses Death Dealer to personally oversee the young Shang-Chi's martial arts training. Death Dealer is a heartless and harsh teacher. Years later, Wenwu sends him to retrieve the pendants he needs to find Ta Lo from Xialing and Shang-Chi.

Long hair tied back

Face mask conceals identity

Wenwu finds the village of Ta Lo and brings his forces with him, including Death Dealer. The warrior is no match for the demonic creatures streaming out of the Dark Gate. They steal Death Dealer's soul.

Padded clothing absorbs impacts

Weapons hidden in robes

REUNION

Years after Shang-Chi escapes his father, he meets Death Dealer again in Macau. He fights his former teacher in a flurry of punches and kicks as old feelings bubble to the surface. Death Dealer is outmatched.

Ornate belt denotes high rank

Reinforced steel bracer

DEADLY SILENT

Death Dealer never utters a word. Whether he's locked in combat with an opponent or witnessing the unbelievable, the stoic fighter stays silent. He lets his actions do the talking.

DATA FILE

AFFILIATION: The Ten Rings, Wenwu
KEY STRENGTHS: Highly trained martial artist, dagger weapons, explosives
APPEARANCES: SCATLOTTR

Peak agility and reflexes

ARISHEM

Prime Celestial

Arishem is the Prime Celestial. He created the first sun and brought light into the universe. Arishem sends immortal heroes called Eternals across the universe, supposedly to protect humanity. Their true purpose is to defend intelligent life on a host planet, until it generates enough energy for a new Celestial to be born. As the Celestial emerges, the planet explodes. When the Eternals on Earth learn the truth, some question Arishem's methods.

CREATION

Arishem explains how he plants the seeds of new Celestials to grow in the cores of host planets. The energy gathered from the host planets is used by the Celestials to form new suns and galaxies. Arishem tells Sersi that the end of one life is the beginning of another.

The Eternals stop the emergence of the Celestial Tiamut to protect Earth. Arishem summons Sersi, Kingo, and Phastos to search their memories and decide if humanity is worth saving.

Body made of cosmic energy

Formation of galaxies and suns

Enormous limbs are larger than a planet

WORLD FORGE

Sersi believes she's from the planet Olympia, but Arishem reveals the truth. The Eternals are synthetic beings. He builds and programs them in the World Forge. Arishem resets their memories after they complete each mission on a host planet.

DATA FILE

AFFILIATION: Celestials, Eternals, Deviants
KEY STRENGTHS: Creation of suns with cosmic energy, interstellar travel, highly advanced technology
APPEARANCES: E

SERSI

Eternal transformation

Sersi is a kindhearted member of the Eternals—immortal beings who protect humanity from monsters known as Deviants. Her super-powers can change the state and makeup of matter, but can't affect sentient beings. After the Deviants' defeat, Sersi parts ways with her husband and fellow Eternal, Ikaris. Many years later, she falls for a human named Dane Whitman, but the reappearance of the Deviants changes everything.

Circular symbols of the Eternals

UNDYING LOVE

Ikaris and Sersi were together for thousands of years. After Ikaris finds out the Eternals' mission will destroy Earth, he leaves Sersi so she doesn't have to learn the truth. Sersi moves on, but the two still have strong feelings for each other.

PRIME ETERNAL

The Prime Eternal, Ajak, chooses Sersi as her successor. The Prime Eternal makes decisions for the group and initiates direct contact with their creator, Arishem. Sersi's love for humanity makes her an ideal leader.

Armor plating protects from Deviant teeth and claws

Team uniform

Sersi uses the shared power of the Eternals, called the Uni-Mind, to transform the living Celestial emerging from Earth's core into stone.

Lightweight boots for evasion and agility

DATA FILE

AFFILIATION: Eternals, Arishem, Dane Whitman, Ikaris
KEY STRENGTHS: Transmutation ability can change makeup of inanimate matter, enhanced strength, agility, stamina, and durability, immortality, communication with Arishem
APPEARANCES: E

IKARIS

Eternal loyalty

The Eternal Ikaris takes his duty very seriously. He believes in their creator, Arishem, and does what it takes to finish their mission. He even permanently silences the Prime Eternal, Ajak, when she shares doubts about allowing the destruction of Earth. Ikaris hides the truth from the other Eternals so that it will be too late to stop the Celestial Tiamut's emergence by the time they find out.

Cosmic energy beams emerge through gaze

Circular symbols of the Eternals

Ikaris provides much of the team's attacking power with forceful energy blasts from his eyes. Combined with the power of flight, Ikaris is a versatile and formidable fighter.

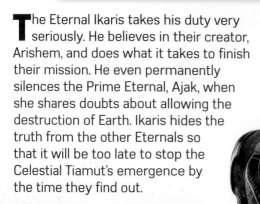

Gilded belt

A LONG HISTORY

Ikaris meets Sersi in 5000 BCE just moments before their ship, the *Domo*, arrives at Earth. He's instantly enchanted. The two Eternals marry in 400 CE. Ikaris and Sersi love each other deeply, but his loyalty to Arishem comes first. Their reunion in present-day London is very tense.

RESOLUTE

Ikaris never questions Arishem's directives. He's willing to attack his fellow Eternals to prevent them from interfering with the emergence of the Celestial Tiamut, even though it means the total annihilation of Earth.

DATA FILE

AFFILIATION: Eternals, Celestials, Arishem, Sersi
KEY STRENGTHS: Flight, energy beams projected from eyes, enhanced strength, agility, stamina, and durability, immortality
APPEARANCES: E

Boots absorb impact when landing

GILGAMESH

Eternal strength

PRANKSTER

Gilgamesh loves to tease the other Eternals, especially Sprite. He jokes about her youthful appearance. She retaliates with her illusion ability to make him look like a baby wearing a bib labeled "Gilga-mess."

Gilgamesh is the mighty powerhouse of the Eternals team. His massive strength is matched only by his compassion—and his love of cooking. Gilgamesh watches over his fellow Eternal Thena as her memories overwhelm her. He risks his own life to care for her. When the Deviants return after thousands of years, he's ready to get back into the fight.

Circular symbols of the Eternals

Uses energy to focus strength or create bracers for defense

PROTECTOR

Gilgamesh defends his remote home in the Australian outback from a snarling Deviant, although it leaves him with wounds after their battle. He's not surprised to see his fellow Eternals on his doorstep shortly after. Gilgamesh takes the news of Ajak's death hard.

Team uniform

In 575 BCE, the Eternals protect the residents of Babylon from multiple Deviants. Gilgamesh holds the city gate and delivers the finishing blow on the leader of the pack.

Boots reinforced at ankles for stability

DATA FILE

AFFILIATION: Eternals, Thena
KEY STRENGTHS: Massive strength, cosmic energy bracers, enhanced agility, stamina, and durability, immortality
APPEARANCES: E

SPRITE

Eternal illusion

Sprite might look like she's the youngest member of the Eternals, but she's the same age as her fellow defenders of Earth. Through the centuries, Sprite stays in touch with Ajak and Sersi. When a Deviant monster attacks in the streets of present-day London, Sprite, Ikaris, and Sersi begin a mission to find the other Eternals and learn why the Deviants returned.

Circular symbols of Eternals

STORYTELLER

While Sprite's power can provide deception and distraction in a fight against a Deviant, she also uses her illusions to tell stories. She projects an image of the Eternals' ship and helps Thena remember their long history together when they meet after a long time apart.

Raised hands focus illusion projections

DATA FILE

AFFILIATION: The Eternals, Sersi, Ikaris
KEY STRENGTHS: Illusion projection, immortality, storytelling
APPEARANCES: E

Team uniform

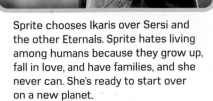

Sprite chooses Ikaris over Sersi and the other Eternals. Sprite hates living among humans because they grow up, fall in love, and have families, and she never can. She's ready to start over on a new planet.

REALIST

Sprite is very practical and tends to be cynical when it comes to humans. Sprite urges Sersi to move in with her boyfriend Dane Whitman soon, since his human life will be short compared to hers.

Flexible boots for all types of Earth terrain

PHASTOS

Eternal innovation

The brilliant inventor Phastos offers humanity technological advances and the inspiration to aid humans in their development. But after seeing his work indirectly lead to terrible war and destruction, the Eternal becomes disillusioned and opts for a quiet life.

Team attire

Wields weapons for offense and defense

LOST AND FOUND

Phastos loses hope in humans after the development of nuclear missiles. They seem too self-destructive to save. Meeting Ben and starting a family together changes his mind, and he finds faith in people again.

Hands manipulate energy constructs of inventions

SIMPLE LIFE

Now going by the name of Phil, Phastos spends his days with his husband, Ben, and their son, Jack. They lead a happy life in the Chicago suburbs. Phastos isn't pleased to see Sersi and Ikaris when they arrive, because he knows it means bad news.

Phastos uses weapons of his own design on both hands. They fire energy blasts, release high-speed metal disks, and can be used as shields.

DATA FILE

AFFILIATION: Eternals, Jack, Ben
KEY STRENGTHS: Superhuman aptitude for technology and invention, highly intelligent, immortality, parenting
APPEARANCES: E

Knee-high boots

DRUIG

Eternal control

One of the Eternals tasked with watching over humanity, Druig is clever and calculating. His ability to control minds is formidable, as is his uncanny insight. He rarely shows emotion. But there is one person Druig has strong feelings for: his fellow Eternal, Makkari.

Team uniform adorned with circle symbols of the Eternals

IMMORTAL AFFECTION

Although they've been apart for hundreds of years, Druig continues to tease Makkari at their reunion. When they're together, they can't take their eyes off each other.

Reinforced clothing for defense during Deviant attacks

IN CHARGE

Druig has kept 20 generations of people in a remote part of the Amazon Forest under his power. He insists it's for protection from the outside world and from themselves. While he doesn't welcome the Eternals into his home warmly, Druig is willing to listen to what they have to say.

Flowing robe gives air of nobility

DATA FILE

AFFILIATION: Eternals, Arishem, Makkari
KEY STRENGTHS: Mind control, immortality, perception, cunning
APPEARANCES: E

While he seems indifferent at first, Druig ultimately risks his life to save the Earth. He plans to use the Eternals' mind link to control the Celestial.

Thick boot soles withstand volcanic ground

MAKKARI

Eternal speed

The swift-footed Eternal Makkari uses her super-speed to protect humans from the threat of dangerous Deviants. While Makkari and Druig share affection for each other, she spends hundreds of years alone collecting historical and cultural artifacts.

Makkari doesn't hold back after Ikaris attacks Druig. Her speed makes her more than a match for him. Ikaris can't dodge her assault.

Decorated with circular symbols of Eternals

Streamlined team uniform with low air resistance

COLLECTOR

Makkari lives on her own on the Eternals' ship, the *Domo*. She chases down important relics from human history— and yummy snacks—and keeps them safe on the ship. She reads books in her collection for fun.

Clothing keeps temperature regulated at all velocities

STRONG SENSES

Makkari can't hear, but she can detect even the tiniest movements by vibrations, including voices. She communicates with the other Eternals through sign language.

Boots crafted to withstand repeated high speeds

DATA FILE

AFFILIATION: Eternals, Druig, Arishem
KEY STRENGTHS: Superhuman speed, immortality, sensing vibrations, artifact acquisition
APPEARANCES: E

KINGO
Eternal energy

Charismatic Kingo is one of the Eternals—cosmic beings on a mission to defend humanity against otherworldly monsters known as Deviants. He's personable and speaks his mind easily. During an era of peace, Kingo dedicates several human life spans to a new career as a movie star in Mumbai, India. He watches out for others, but he also tends to look out for himself as well.

Circular symbols of the Eternals

STORIED PAST

Kingo uses the Eternals' long history of adventures as inspiration for his Bollywood movies. His latest project is a film based on the legendary exploits of Ikaris.

Lightweight armor protects against Deviant attacks

DYNASTY

A movie star for over 100 years, Kingo pretended to be his own great-great-grandfather and then subsequent generations of actors to avoid suspicion. He adores the spotlight and cares for the people he works with.

Confident stance

Kingo releases bursts of cosmic energy to fight the Deviants. He fires powerful projectiles from his hands and fingers to stop the monsters in their tracks.

DATA FILE

AFFILIATION: Eternals, Karun Patel, Arishem, Bollywood
KEY STRENGTHS: Cosmic energy projection, immortality, charm, charisma
APPEARANCES: E

KARUN PATEL

Devoted valet

Karun Patel started working with Kingo 50 years ago. Convinced the immortal Eternal was a vampire, Karun attempted to stake Kingo through the heart—something he's still embarrassed about. Karun is now fully aware of Kingo's history as an Eternal and is thrilled to meet his heroic teammates.

Tries to keep
a steady hand
when filming

Cross-body
bag packed
with filming
equipment

GREAT HONOR

Karun recognizes how much the Eternals have done for humanity and considers them Earth's original Super Heroes. He chooses to stay with them and be at their sides for the fight against the Deviants, despite the obvious danger.

DATA FILE

AFFILIATION: Kingo, Eternals
KEY STRENGTHS: Loyalty, wisdom, preparation, camerawork
APPEARANCES: E

ONLY HUMAN

He may not be an Eternal, but Karun's wisdom is still extraordinary. He appreciates the beauty in life, even in a creature as monstrous as a Deviant. Karun gently encourages Druig to keep his hope in humanity.

Ever prepared, Karun brings several cameras to film Kingo's documentary about the Eternals. He's determined to get some action-packed shots.

DANE WHITMAN
Charming historian

Dane Whitman is an easygoing member of the staff at the Natural History Museum. He falls in love with Sersi, a teacher at the museum. Dane wonders if she's a sorcerer because strange things happen around her. The sudden appearance of an aggressive Deviant creature confirms his suspicions. Sersi reveals that she and her "niece" Sprite are Eternals.

COMPLICATED HISTORY

Dane tells Sersi he has a secret of his own in his family history. Later, he hears a mysterious black sword in his office whispering to him, but he's interrupted just before he touches it.

Warm scarf for chilly London days

Casual but stylish jacket

Dane can only stand by and watch as Ikaris takes on a massive Deviant in the streets of London. He encourages bystanders to get to safety.

IN LOVE

Even when Sersi reveals she's hundreds of years old and comes from the planet Olympia, Dane's feelings for her don't change. He jokes that he's sad only that she isn't a wizard. When she says she can no longer pretend to be human, Dane declares he loves her and doesn't care who she is.

DATA FILE

AFFILIATION: Natural History Museum, Sersi, Sprite
KEY STRENGTHS: History, science, poetry, open-mindedness, complicated family history
APPEARANCES: E

KRO

Deviant leader

A rishem created the Deviants to protect humans from predators, but the Deviants evolved into predators themselves. Centuries after the Eternals eliminate the monsters from Earth, the planet's core begins to heat up. This frees the remaining Deviants from their icy imprisonment in an Alaskan glacier. The Deviant Kro absorbs Ajak's powers, transforming his body and mind in a metamorphosis.

SURVIVAL

Kro is driven by rage against the Eternals, Celestials, and Arishem. With each emergence of a Celestial, countless lives are lost, including those of Deviants. Kro says they simply want to survive.

REVENGE

Kro absorbs the massive strength and energy of Gilgamesh. It causes him to evolve into a more humanlike form, capable of thought and speech. He finally understands the memories he stole from Ajak. Kro swears revenge on the Eternals for hunting his kind.

Tentacles absorb Eternals' cosmic energy

With the cosmic energy he absorbed from Ajak and Gilgamesh, Kro can withstand a combined attack from Makkari and Phastos. Thena bests him in one final fight.

DATA FILE

AFFILIATION: Deviants
KEY STRENGTHS: Monstrous strength, regeneration, and durability, command over lesser Deviants, absorption of Eternals' energy, memories, and abilities
APPEARANCES: E

Capable of accelerated self-healing

PIP THE TROLL
Herald of Eros

Disheveled hair

Pip the Troll teleports onto the Eternals' ship, the *Domo*, with a flash of colors and a belly flop. He announces the arrival of Eros, the brother of Thanos, with a lot of flair (and possibly a burp). Thena, Druig, and Makkari don't know what to make of the unusual but friendly pair.

HYPE MAN
Pip introduces Eros by listing his many adventurous exploits. He gets a couple of the details wrong, but Pip's admiration for his friend is obvious. They have a long history together.

Padded gloves for messy landings after teleporting

Some of the Eternals of Earth have been missing for weeks. Pip and Eros offer the others their help in finding them.

Comfortable jerkin

Ornate detailing

DRAMATIC ENTRANCE
Confident Pip seems to enjoy being the center of attention on arrival, but he also happily shares the spotlight with Eros.

DATA FILE
AFFILIATION: Eros
KEY STRENGTHS: Introductions
APPEARANCES: E

Favorite drink in hand

KATE BISHOP

Plucky archer

Kate Bishop was just a girl when the Avengers fought the Chitauri in New York City. Debris from the battle fell on her family's penthouse and mortally injured her father. She glimpsed Clint Barton in action through the dust. The brave, bow-slinging Avenger made a huge impression on her. Kate began training in archery. Years later, when she unintentionally steals the Ronin suit from an auction, she comes face-to-face with her hero, Hawkeye.

Kate and Clint fire arrows side by side. Countless members of the Tracksuit Mafia rush them, but the mentor and student work seamlessly together. The Tracksuits are no match for the daring duo.

Tactical holster holds quiver

FIGHTER

Kate is a college student when she meets Clint. She's only 22 years old but is already an experienced fighter. Kate started training in martial arts when she was 5 and earned her black belt at 15.

Costume designed by role-player Missy

Bracer protects inner arm from bowstring

Belt stores additional arrowheads

Trick arrow

GLITZY PARTY

Kate tags along with her mom, Eleanor, to a high-society charity auction. During the party, she comes across the distinguished Armand Dusquesne, whom she met as a child. Shortly after, Kate stumbles upon Armand's body, involving her in a mystery that will forever change her life.

DATA FILE

AFFILIATION: Eleanor Bishop, Clint Barton, Lucky the Pizza Dog
KEY STRENGTHS: Highly trained in martial arts, archery, fencing, and gymnastics, trick arrows, bravery
APPEARANCES: H

LUCKY THE PIZZA DOG

Golden boy

Kate Bishop spots a stray dog on the sidewalk one night, who gazes back at her with just one eye. Shortly after, Kate sees the dog dart into traffic, and she jumps between the oncoming cars to save him. She brings him home and feeds him the only food she has— leftover pizza. The stray gobbles it down and becomes an instant fan of pizza—and Kate.

Long silky ears

Clint Barton cares about Pizza Dog more than he wants to admit. He worries the unnamed dog is too cooped up inside their hideout, so Clint insists on taking him on their outings. Pizza Dog enjoys walkies.

Festive hat

FRIENDLY EAR

Kate cleans up the dog and gets him a collar and leash. Pizza Dog is a good listener, and Kate often finds herself talking to him. She sounds out her thoughts about her current predicament as they walk together in the park.

Good dog

PET NAME

Deciding on the pup's name isn't easy. Kate tries out Little Ol' Caesar, Dogfather, and Sir Dog of Pizza. "Pizza Dog" is close, but later Kate reveals the name she finally picked: Lucky.

DATA FILE

AFFILIATION: Kate Bishop, Clint Barton
KEY STRENGTHS: Loyalty, luck
APPEARANCES: H

MAYA LOPEZ

Vengeful fighter

Maya Lopez grew up closely watching the world around her. Maya is deaf and uses a prosthetic leg. As a child, she honed her observation skills to read a person's lips—and to predict the moves they're about to make. Through training and hard work, Maya became a skilled hand-to-hand fighter. She loses her father, leader of the Tracksuit Mafia, at the hands of the vigilante Ronin. Maya swears revenge. She takes her father's place and is determined to find Ronin.

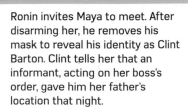

Ronin invites Maya to meet. After disarming her, he removes his mask to reveal his identity as Clint Barton. Clint tells her that an informant, acting on her boss's order, gave him her father's location that night.

Padded leather tracksuit jacket absorbs hits

Fast reflexes from training in karate, boxing, and more since childhood

SINGLE-MINDED
Maya questions Clint Barton and Kate Bishop about the Ronin suit. She doesn't believe Clint's statement that Ronin is dead, and she has no patience for Kate's flippant attitude. Maya wants answers and will do whatever it takes to get them.

UNCLE
Ever since she was a girl, Maya's "uncle" Wilson Fisk has supported her. Fisk, known in the underworld as Kingpin, genuinely cares for Maya. He sees that she's turned against him, though she tries to hide it.

DATA FILE

AFFILIATION: William Lopez, Tracksuit Mafia, Kazi, Kingpin

KEY STRENGTHS: Highly trained in martial arts, observation, determination

APPEARANCES: H

WILSON FISK

Kingpin

Wilson Fisk, known as the Kingpin in the underworld, is at the top of the Tracksuit Mafia and other organizations in his criminal empire. Kingpin has a menacing manner, which gives the impression that uncontrollable fury is brimming just beneath the surface. He believes that New York City belongs to him. Fisk and his shady business dealings have long been in the sights of the Avenger Clint Barton.

Eleanor Bishop begins working with Kingpin, in order to repay the small fortune her late husband owed him. Both benefit financially from their relationship, but Eleanor severs ties as her daughter, Kate, gets close to learning about their arrangement. Kingpin is furious.

Intimidating snarl

Fond of clean white suit jackets

Walking cane doubles as weapon

STRONGMAN

When Kingpin goes after Eleanor Bishop, her daughter intervenes. Kate hits him directly in the chest with an arrow. It has no effect. Kingpin and Kate fight, and he easily overpowers her with his tremendous strength. It takes all of her explosive trick arrows at once to knock him unconscious.

DATA FILE

AFFILIATION: Tracksuit Mafia, Maya Lopez, Eleanor Bishop
KEY STRENGTHS: Underworld resources and contacts, strength and durability
APPEARANCES: H

FAMILY

Fisk's gentler side comes out only when he's talking to Maya Lopez. He has cared for Maya since she was a little girl. Fisk learns some sign language over the years so they can communicate directly.

ELEANOR BISHOP

Misguided mom

Eleanor and Derek Bishop, Kate's parents, didn't always see eye to eye. When Derek died in the Chitauri attack on New York City, Eleanor decided to do whatever was needed to protect Kate and herself. She successfully turned their fortunes around, but at the cost of doing business with the criminal Kingpin. Her life becomes intertwined with Kingpin's shady dealings—and so does Kate's.

Ruby-red designer gown

DRAW THE LINE

Eleanor is practical and decisive. She does what she is told to repay her husband's debt to Kingpin but refuses to let her daughter get close to that world. However, Kingpin won't let Eleanor end their business relationship.

TOUGH LOVE

Eleanor and Kate often argue, but it's because Eleanor wants what she thinks is best for Kate. She hopes to see Kate follow in her footsteps at Bishop Security and promises it will make her happy. But her daughter isn't so sure it's the life she wants.

Sparkling engagement ring

Jack Duquesne unabashedly adores Eleanor. She obviously doesn't feel the same way and follows the Kingpin's orders to make Jack take the blame for the murder of his uncle, Armand Duquesne.

DATA FILE

AFFILIATION: Bishop Security, Kate Bishop, Jack Duquesne, Wilson Fisk
KEY STRENGTHS: Pragmatism, management, deception
APPEARANCES: H

JACK DUQUESNE

Smooth talker

Jack Duquesne is right at home at a fancy party. He feels just as comfortable in a tuxedo as most people do in sweatpants. Jack is marrying the wealthy Eleanor Bishop, much to her daughter Kate's surprise. He's madly in love with Eleanor, but Kate can't shake the feeling that Jack seems to be hiding something.

WHIRLWIND ROMANCE

The undeniably charming Jack sweeps Eleanor off her feet, and the relationship moves quickly from there. He moves in and proposes to Eleanor before Kate has a chance to find out about them.

Tailored vest

SWORDSMAN

Jack collects unusual swords. In an underground auction, he bids on a one-of-a-kind retractable sword that belonged to the vigilante Ronin. He can't resist stealing it in a moment of chaos.

Twill dress shirt

While he makes some bad decisions, Jack genuinely cares for Eleanor and Kate. He fights to protect Kate from bad guys.

DATA FILE

AFFILIATION: Eleanor Bishop, Kate Bishop
KEY STRENGTHS: Sword fighting, charm, charisma, perception
APPEARANCES: H

Leather gloves for sword grip and injury prevention

Battered but beloved sword from personal collection

Scabbard

AMERICA CHAVEZ

Portal powerhouse

America Chavez has the unique ability to travel between universes. As a girl, she was unable to control her power and accidentally opened a portal that tossed her moms and herself out into the Multiverse. She never saw them again. America is traveling between universes and trying to find her way home when The Scarlet Witch sets her sights on America's power and seeks to claim it.

Hand-painted denim jacket

Able to punch open star-shaped portals to other universes

WELL-TRAVELED
After visiting more than 70 different universes, America has learned a few things. She tells Doctor Strange that the first rule of Multiverse travel is that you don't know anything. No two universes are alike.

SUPREME PIZZA
America sits down with Doctor Strange and Sorcerer Supreme Wong for a quick slice of pizza. She tells them that a Doctor Strange from another universe was looking for the Book of Vishanti—a mythical tome of good magic—to defeat a creature chasing America through the Multiverse.

DATA FILE
AFFILIATION: The Multiverse, Doctor Strange, Wong, Kamar-Taj
KEY STRENGTHS: Multiversal travel, resilience, survival instincts, bravery
APPEARANCES: DSITMOM

After a pep talk from Doctor Strange, the teen realizes she can control her super-powers. America opens a star-shaped portal to Kamar-Taj so she and Wong can escape from Mount Wundagore.

Sneakers for quick getaways

DEFENDER STRANGE

Desperate doctor

Defender Strange is a Doctor Strange from another universe. He helps Multiverse traveler America Chavez outrun the monstrous creature chasing her and traps the wriggling monster in a spell—but realizes that his magic won't hold it in place for long. Defender Strange makes the devastating decision to take America's power for safekeeping. The creature kills him before the spell is complete.

Long hair gathered in a ponytail

Defender Strange dies, but his body is given a new life—sort of. Doctor Strange possesses his corpse while Dreamwalking from a different universe. The dead, however, are not pleased about his trespassing in another realm.

Mystical robes

ON THE RUN

Defender Strange and America Chavez race toward the powerful Book of Vishanti. It's hidden in the Gap Junction, the space between universes. The demonic monster catches up to them before they can reach the book.

Casts spells that glow with silvery energy

GREATER GOOD

Defender Strange tries to steal America's Multiverse power, but he's not a villain. With his last breath, he flings magical weapons that slice through the creature's tentacles, freeing America from its clutches. She gets away safely.

Gold belt loop

DATA FILE

AFFILIATION: Masters of the Mystic Arts, America Chavez
KEY STRENGTHS: Training and study of the mystic arts, spellcasting, multilingual, quick thinking
APPEARANCES: DSITMOM

Leaps far distances with magic

838-BARON MORDO

Secretive Sorcerer Supreme

Baron Karl Mordo is the Sorcerer Supreme of Universe-838. He's not surprised to see a Doctor Strange from another universe on the Sanctum's doorstep. Unlike the man Doctor Strange knows in his world, this Mordo has no ill feelings for him. However, Mordo considers anyone from another universe a potential threat to his reality.

DATA FILE

AFFILIATION: The Illuminati, Masters of the Mystic Arts, New York Sanctum
KEY STRENGTHS: Casting spells, hand-to-hand combat
APPEARANCES: DSITMOM

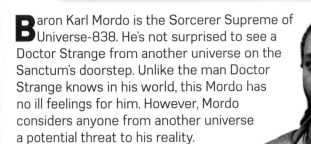

Ornate robes befitting the Sorcerer Supreme

Silk sash

SECRET SOCIETY

As Sorcerer Supreme, Mordo is a member of The Illuminati. The super-secret organization was created by the Doctor Strange of Universe-838 to make difficult decisions that no one else can.

WARM WELCOME

While Mordo welcomes Doctor Strange and America Chavez with a smile, he can't risk their presence triggering a collision of their universes. He uses the Sands of Nisanti to put them to sleep and takes them to The Illuminati.

Mordo believes another universe's Doctor Strange is more dangerous than The Scarlet Witch. He doesn't intend on letting Strange leave The Illuminati headquarters.

Vaulting Boots of Valtorr

Heavy cloak

838-WANDA MAXIMOFF

Multiverse mom

Wanda Maximoff of Universe-838 lives a happy life with her two young sons, Billy and Tommy. It's the life The Scarlet Witch literally dreams of, and she'll do anything to have it for herself. Corrupted by the Darkhold book's influence, The Scarlet Witch intends to steal America Chavez's power to travel through the Multiverse and take Wanda's place in Universe-838.

Anxious expression

EXTRAORDINARY

While Wanda of Universe-838 wields the same formidable powers as The Scarlet Witch, she isn't a spell-slinging member of The Illuminati. Wanda lives life in a quiet neighborhood with her children.

TRAPPED

The Scarlet Witch Dreamwalks in Wanda's body. When the witch is in control, Wanda is imprisoned within her own mind. It feels like she's caught beneath rubble. Not even the considerable mental powers of Illuminati member Professor Charles Xavier can free Wanda from the spell.

Cozy clothes for relaxed home life

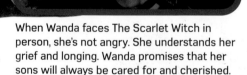

When Wanda faces The Scarlet Witch in person, she's not angry. She understands her grief and longing. Wanda promises that her sons will always be cared for and cherished.

DATA FILE

AFFILIATION: Billy Maximoff, Tommy Maximoff
KEY STRENGTHS: Telekinesis, telepathy, Chaos Magic, compassion
APPEARANCES: DSITMOM

838-CAPTAIN CARTER

The first Avenger

In Universe-838, Peggy Carter takes the place of Steve Rogers in the Project Rebirth experiment. The Super Soldier Serum is a success, and the British agent gains superhuman strength and a peak physical condition. Captain Carter defends the Earth against all threats—even if one of them is a friend.

Jetpack capable of short bursts of flight

Vibranium shield with the Union Flag

DEFENDING THE UNIVERSE

As leader of Universe-838's Avengers, Captain Carter is a member of The Illuminati. She's willing to do whatever it takes to keep her reality safe from Doctor Strange, no matter how difficult the choice is.

DAUNTLESS

Like Steve Rogers, it's hard to keep Captain Carter down. No matter how many hits her opponent lands, she always gets back up to keep fighting for what she believes in.

Longtime teammates Captain Carter and Captain Marvel stand together when The Scarlet Witch breaches The Illuminati headquarters. Unfortunately, they make the disastrous mistake of underestimating Wanda Maximoff.

DATA FILE

AFFILIATION:
The Illuminati, Universe-838
KEY STRENGTHS:
Superhuman strength, agility, and endurance, flight (with jetpack), leadership, determination
APPEARANCES:
DSITMOM

Reinforced uniform protects against most standard attacks

Broken-in leather combat boots

Able to throw shield with pinpoint accuracy

838-DR. CHRISTINE PALMER

Sympathetic scientist

Dr. Christine Palmer of Universe-838 works within a secret foundation to research the Multiverse. She monitors visitors from other worlds before they have a chance to become a threat. Christine holds Doctor Strange and America Chavez captive in a research facility. She later decides to help them, despite the danger to her own world.

Christine keeps her cool no matter what happens. She protects Doctor Strange from angry spirits with the Brazier of Bom'Galiath.

COMPLICATED

Christine has a rocky relationship with Strange in almost every universe. In Universe-838, Christine lost her Stephen Strange. She still has affection for this unfamiliar Doctor Strange, even if he comes from another universe.

Crisp research team uniform

Baxter Foundation ID card

DATA FILE

AFFILIATION: Baxter Foundation, The Illuminati, Doctor Strange
KEY STRENGTHS: High intelligence, science and technology, multiversal research, courage
APPEARANCES: DSITMOM

INVENTOR

In Universe-838, Christine worked with her Stephen Strange to combine the mystic arts with science and technology. They developed a magic inhibitor that prevents the captive Doctor Strange from casting spells to escape.

SINISTER STRANGE

Corrupted sorcerer

Sinister Strange is the sole resident of a New York City in which two realities collided—a cataclysmic event known as an Incursion. Doctor Strange and the Dr. Christine Palmer of Universe-838 make their way through the eerily silent city streets to the Sanctum. Inside, Doctor Strange meets Sinister Strange, a mistrustful version of himself who risked everything for happiness—and lost it all.

Sinister Strange watches Christine from his Sanctum's window. He broke his reality trying to find a universe where he and Christine had a happy life together.

FACING THE MUSIC

Doctor Strange and Sinister Strange duel with magical music notes as sharp-edged weapons. Sinister Strange's spells are cast with a menacing purple energy, in contrast to Doctor Strange's bright gold magic. Sinister Strange loses the orchestral clash.

Unkempt robe of Mystic Arts

HEAVY TOLL

As the Darkhold corrupts Sinister Strange, he decides to end the misery of the unhappy versions of himself he encounters in the Multiverse. Its dark magic also bestows him with an unsettling third eye.

DATA FILE

AFFILIATION: New York Sanctum, Darkhold
KEY STRENGTHS: Master of the Mystic Arts, spellcasting, Darkhold magic
APPEARANCES: DSITMOM

The Darkhold

CLEA

Unexpected visitor

Doctor Strange hears his name called out one chilly fall morning. He turns to see a mysterious white-haired woman, dressed in purple, standing on the New York City sidewalk. Her name is Clea. She coldly tells Doctor Strange that he caused an Incursion in another universe, and he needs to fix it.

CRYPTIC MYSTIC

While Clea obviously knows who Doctor Strange is, she doesn't reveal anything about herself. Doctor Strange is quick to take her at her word and jumps through the portal at her side.

Lightweight armor for Multiverse travel

DARK DIMENSION

A glowing blade appears in Clea's hand, and she uses it to cut a tear in reality. Another dimension is visible beyond the portal she rips open.

DATA FILE

AFFILIATION: Doctor Strange
KEY STRENGTHS: Unknown
APPEARANCES: DSITMOM

Clea faces the portal she opened and waits for Doctor Strange to join her. Strange magically suits up, changing into his mystic robes and donning the Cloak of Levitation.

KAMALA KHAN

Ms. Marvel

NAMED AFTER
Kamala's chosen hero name is inspired by her own favorite hero—Captain Marvel. But it has deeper meaning as well: the "Kamal" in Kamala means "wonder" or "marvel" in the Urdu language.

Mask keeps secret identity safe

Symbol from favorite necklace

Suit designed by Kamala's mom

Teenager Kamala Khan discovers her powers when she puts on a bangle that once belonged to her great-grandmother, Aisha. Kamala finds out that Aisha was displaced from the Noor dimension. The bangle allows Kamala to harness the power of the Noor energy and turn it into light constructs that are powerful enough to catch a truck or stop bullets.

Bangle unlocks energy from another dimension

Kamala wears a homemade Captain Marvel costume to AvengerCon. When her powers suddenly manifest at the convention, she can't control them. Her loyal friend Bruno helps her understand her new abilities.

DATA FILE

AFFILIATION: Jersey City, Noor Dimension
KEY STRENGTHS: Creating energy constructs, encyclopedic knowledge of Super Heroes, support network of family and friends
APPEARANCES: MM, TM

Lightweight shoes for skipping across energy constructs

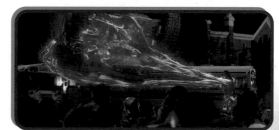

STRONG COMMUNITY
Kamala's powers are mighty, but her relationship with her network of friends and family is just as powerful. Members of her local community and her mosque also cheer on their hometown heroine as she saves them from a falling vehicle.

BRUNO CARELLI

Brainy BFF

Bruno Carelli is one of Kamala Khan's best friends. A high-school student with a gift for science, Bruno is practically part of her family. He is always there for Kamala when she needs help, especially when he finds out she has new super-powers.

Concerned expression

Bruno offers a helping hand as Kamala takes her first steps as a Super Hero. She gingerly steps down onto a hard light construct, and he catches her as it gives way.

GIFTED RESEARCHER

Kamala explores her new abilities with Bruno's scientific guidance. He tests her powers, researches inter-dimensional travel, and examines her genetic make-up for clues.

Dressed in lab coat as his favorite hero, Dr. Bruce Banner

Day pass to AvengerCon

DATA FILE

AFFILIATION: Kamala Khan, Jersey City
KEY STRENGTHS: High intelligence, science and technology, research skills, dependability
APPEARANCES: MM

CRUSHING

Bruno's feelings for Kamala are obvious to everyone else but her. Even though he's jealous of the boy Kamala likes, Bruno still does everything that he can to help him.

NAKIA BAHADIR

Fearless friend

Best friends Nakia Bahadir and Kamala Khan tell each other everything. They're so close, they even share a secret handshake. But after Nakia complains about the new Super Hero bringing too much attention to their mosque, Kamala decides to hide her new abilities. Nakia catches a glimpse of her powers in action at the Khan family wedding, and she's instantly hurt that Kamala didn't trust her with the truth.

ADVOCATE

Whether it's a dodgeball thrown too hard during PE or a secret government agency chasing super-powered teens, Nakia stands up to anyone who comes after her friends.

Statement earrings

Warm coat combined with colorful turtleneck

ACTIVIST

Eager to make a difference, Nakia runs for the Mosque Board election with Kamala's full support. Nakia wants to improve the women's area of the mosque. She campaigns during the Eid celebration and talks Kamala's father, Yusuf, into voting for her. Nakia is proud to win a hard-earned place on the board.

Nakia doesn't like Super Heroes, but she's upset that her best friend didn't tell her about her powers. Kamala admits she was afraid of how Nakia might react.

DATA FILE

AFFILIATION: Kamala Khan, Bruno Carelli, Ms. Marvel
KEY STRENGTHS: Activism, bravery
APPEARANCES: MM

THE KHAN FAMILY

Heroic household

Muneeba and Yusuf Khan are the loving parents of Aamir and Kamala Khan. The Khan family are part of a close-knit Pakistani community in Jersey City and are respected members of their mosque. The family is getting ready for the upcoming wedding of Aamir and Tyesha when an aged bangle unlocks Kamala's light-based energy powers. When Muneeba, Yusuf, Aamir, and Tyesha find out Kamala is the new local Super Hero, they do everything they can to support her, even if it means trouble with the authorities.

CELEBRATION

The wedding of Aamir Khan and Tyesha Hillman is a joyous ceremony followed by a reception filled with dancing and laughter. Kamala pulls the fire alarm when she realizes that wedding crashers from the Noor Dimension will hurt everyone in attendance. Yusuf and Muneeba aren't happy.

Aamir surprises Kamala at the high school while they go over the plan to deal with the Department of Damage Control agents waiting outside. Their mom sent him to the school to watch out for his sister.

Muneeba and her mother, Sana, have a strained relationship. Sana knows about the bangle connected to Kamala's powers and helps her understand its history in their family.

Keeps a secret stash of cherry pies

Big fan of Earth's biggest heroes

Upcoming wedding on his mind

PROUD PARENTS

Yusuf and Muneeba don't understand everything that Kamala gets excited about, including her love of Super Heroes. But they always try their hardest to encourage her in every endeavor—especially when Kamala becomes a Super Hero herself.

Colorful floral print

DATA FILE

AFFILIATION: Tyesha Hillman, Bruno Carelli, Nakia Bahadir, Jersey City

KEY STRENGTHS: Unity, faith, courage, strong community, bilingual in Urdu and English

APPEARANCES: MM, TM

KAMRAN
Conflicted Clandestine

Kamran is a new student who makes a big splash when Kamala Khan sees him for the first time. Kamran emerges from a swimming pool and introduces himself to her. When police interrupt the party, he gives Kamala and her friends a ride home. While he seems like a typical teenager, Kamran is hiding a secret of his own: his mother, Najma, and her ageless associates, the Clandestines, come from another dimension.

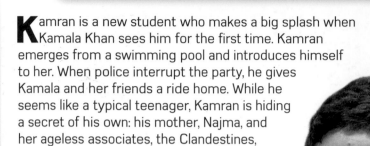

When Najma sacrifices herself to close a rift to the Noor Dimension, the resulting energy connects to Kamran. He gains hard light projection abilities like Kamala's, but he can't control them.

Warm coat for cold New Jersey nights

Stylish T-shirt

CHARMER

Kamran and Kamala feel an immediate connection, although her best friend Bruno isn't a fan. They hang out for a fun afternoon together. Later, Kamran introduces Kamala to his mother, who reveals that she's from the Noor Dimension. They need Kamala's power to help them get home.

TOUGH CHOICE

Kamran finds out that Najma knows Earth will be destroyed if they return to the Noor Dimension. He goes against his mom to warn Kamala that she and her family are in danger. He fights against the Clandestines when they come after her.

DATA FILE

AFFILIATION: Najma, Clandestines, Noor Dimension, Bruno Carelli
KEY STRENGTHS: Ability to project hard light, charisma, nice car
APPEARANCES: MM

KING YAKAN

Stunned sovereign

King Yakan is the ruler of Indigarr. Its warmongering archenemies, the Booskans, threaten his people. Thor and the Guardians of the Galaxy find themselves smack in the middle of their war. Yakan is relieved to see the legendary God of Thunder, but not everything goes according to plan.

Royal headdress

King Yakan is flabbergasted when the God of Thunder destroys the temple along with Habooska. The king gives Thor two giant screaming goats as his "reward."

Accessories made of fine fabric and precious metal

Shining silklike robes

SACRED SHRINE

The Indigarrians' gods have been defeated. Yakan tells Thor their unguarded holy temple is now occupied by Habooska the Horrible and his horde of followers. Yakan is offended by their presence inside. He looks forward to Thor striking the final blow against his foes—but the Asgardian wants to deliver a rousing speech first.

Long sleeves follow high fashion on Indigarr

DATA FILE

AFFILIATION: Indigarr, Thor, Guardians of the Galaxy
KEY STRENGTHS: Planetary royalty
APPEARANCES: T:LAI

PEACEFUL OASIS

Yakan's home planet of Indigarr is beautiful when it's not under siege. Three suns and a ringed planet hang low in the golden sky at the end of the day. Thor takes a moment to admire the resplendent skyscape before joining the battle.

HABOOSKA THE HORRIBLE

Daring warmonger

Habooska the Horrible and his horde of Booskans take advantage of the chaos after the gods of Indigarr are slain. They claim Indigarr's most sacred temple as their own and use it as a base to wage war. Habooska battles the Guardians of the Galaxy and the planet's defense forces from their strategic position.

FALL BACK

Thor rips through the temple and knocks Habooska off his perch. He falls to the ground below. The Booskan forces scatter after the loss of their leader. The Indigarrians are thrilled—then horrified a few seconds later as the glittering temple shatters into pieces.

Hair ruffled by high winds at top of temple

ROOST

Habooska the Horrible occupies the highest point of the temple. He has the perfect vantage point for firing a barrage of laser blasts on the Indigarrian fighters below.

The Booskans might have heavy vehicles and an arsenal of explosive weapons, but they're still no match for the God of Thunder and his axe, Stormbreaker.

Knotted and braided hair

DATA FILE

AFFILIATION: Booskans
KEY STRENGTHS:
Long-range weaponry, heavy vehicles, Booskan army
APPEARANCES: T:LAT

JENNIFER WALTERS

She-Hulk

Jennifer Walters is a lawyer for the District Attorney's office. She has a famous cousin: Bruce Banner, the Hulk. When a car accident mixes some of Bruce's irradiated blood with her own, Jennifer (Jen) transforms into the mighty powerhouse She-Hulk. And that's just the start of her troubles! From high-stakes battles in the courtroom to dealing with her overbearing family, She-Hulk has her hands full.

6 ft 7 in (2 m) tall when in She-Hulk state

Strength matches the Hulk

PUBLIC DEFENDER

Jen is a Super Hero, but she doesn't want to give up her legal career. She takes a new job at the law firm GLK&H, specializing in superhuman-related cases. Thanks to her work, Jen meets some big-time Super Villains and Super Heroes, including Abomination and Wong, the Sorcerer Supreme.

Suit by Luke Jacobson fits both Jen and She-Hulk

GAMMA-POWERED

Jen's transformation is caused by gamma radiation. Unlike Bruce, Jen is in full control of changing between forms. She chooses when to become She-Hulk. Jen also maintains her personality when she Hulks out.

Legs capable of leaping long distances

DATA FILE

AFFILIATION: Hulk, GLK&H, Nikki Ramos
KEY STRENGTHS: Superhuman strength, durability, speed, and regeneration, legal expertise
APPEARANCES: SH:AAL

Bruce gives Jen a crash course in being a Hulk. It includes meditation, balance, and learning to use her massive strength. Jen masters her new Hulk powers quickly, to Bruce's surprise.

Prefers to wear shoes, unlike her cousin

NIKKI RAMOS

Bold bestie

Nikki Ramos is a bright paralegal who works with Jennifer Walters, aka She-Hulk. She joins Jen in their new jobs in the superhuman division at the law firm GLK&H in Los Angeles. Not only is Nikki one of the finest legal assistants around, but she's also one of the best friends anyone can have.

Eye-catching accessories

Inquisitive and perceptive mind

FEARLESS

Nikki decides to infiltrate the online group harassing She-Hulk. It's a risky move. She may not have super-powers, but Nikki is willing to put herself in danger if it means helping a friend.

Keeps up with fashion trends

BFF

Whether it's a legal case or a big gala to get dressed up for, Nikki is always there for Jen. Finding out that Jen is a Hulk didn't change how Nikki sees her best friend. She still delivers the brutal honesty Jen needs now and again without any fear that her BFF will Hulk out on her. That's a sign of true friendship.

Loves a pop of color

DATA FILE

AFFILIATION: She-Hulk, Augustus "Pug" Pugliese, GLK&H
KEY STRENGTHS: Organization, attention to detail, research, loyalty, support
APPEARANCES: SH:AAL

Comfortable but chic ankle boots

Jen might not be concerned about the negative attention she's getting online, but Nikki is. She discovers a creepy website called Intelligencia is targeting She-Hulk.

AUGUSTUS "PUG" PUGLIESE

Considerate counselor

Augustus Pugliese, who goes by the nickname "Pug," is a lawyer at the firm GLK&H. He welcomes Jen Walters and Nikki Ramos to the superhuman law division with a big smile and an overstuffed gift basket. His thoughtfulness makes an instant impression, and they quickly become firm friends.

Cheerful grin

From helping Nikki locate a hard-to-find tailor for She-Hulk to attending an award ceremony to cheer for Jen, Pug supports his friends.

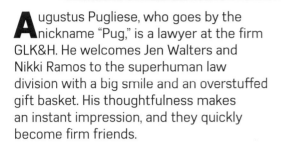

Expertly tied necktie

GOOD GUY

When Nikki contacts the online group threatening She-Hulk, Pug goes to their meetup on her behalf. He has trouble fitting in with the narrow-minded, insecure men at the event.

Gift basket includes a map to the best bathroom in the office

DATA FILE

AFFILIATION: She-Hulk, Nikki Ramos, GLK&H
KEY STRENGTHS: Legal expertise, support, gift baskets
APPEARANCES: SH:AAL

LIMITED EDITIONS

Pug is a sneakerhead. He asks Nikki to go with him to buy the newest Iron Man Three shoes. He wants one pair to wear and one to keep in his collection.

TITANIA

Bad influencer

Titania explodes through a courtroom wall just as lawyer Jennifer Walters is getting ready to make closing remarks in a case. The two become instant enemies. While Titania has the strength to match She-Hulk, she prefers to fight another way: through licensing and copyright.

Perfectly coiffed hair

LIKE AND SUBSCRIBE

Titania may be devious, but her products and social media are wildly successful. She's an expert at marketing her own likeness and knows just how to capture an audience.

Always on the lookout for new ways to promote herself, Titania releases her own cosmetics line. Stealing She-Hulk's name and suing Jen in court for trademark misuse makes it all the more fun.

Eye-catching statement piece

Expensive crystal-embellished corset

Shimmering leggings

PUBLIC HUMILIATION

Jen Walters wins against Titania in court, but their fight isn't over yet. Titania crashes Jen's friend's wedding for a highly visible rematch against She-Hulk. While she usually revels in attention, this time Titania gets a lot more than she bargained for.

DATA FILE

AFFILIATION: She-Hulk
KEY STRENGTHS: Superhuman strength and durability, self-promotion, merchandise
APPEARANCES: SH:AAL

Sequined boots

SKAAR

Son of Hulk

While Jen Walters is having her first big adventure as She-Hulk, Bruce Banner is called away to deal with an urgent matter on Sakaar. He arrives back on Earth just in time for the family picnic. He introduces everyone to someone he has brought with him: his son, Skaar.

Fashionable hairstyle on Sakaar

Same scowl as his father

DATA FILE

AFFILIATION: Hulk, She-Hulk, Sakaar
KEY STRENGTHS: Unknown
APPEARANCES: SH:AAL

WELCOME

Bruce and Jen's family can be nosy and a little tactless. But they're also open-minded, especially when it comes to Hulks. They immediately welcome Skaar into the fold with open arms.

CULTURE SHOCK

Skaar greets his extended family without a word or even a smile. He doesn't know what to make of the boisterous Banners and Walters. How will Skaar react to the unpredictable people of a planet as strange as Earth?

Hulk once spent time on Sakaar as a gladiator. Bruce responds to a message to return to Sakaar, where he meets his son for the first time.

ANEKA
Midnight Angel

Aneka is a member of Wakanda's royal guard. She goes undercover at the Wakandan Outreach Center to stop a vibranium robbery. Smart and resourceful, Aneka is fond of the energy daggers Shuri invented for her but just as skilled with the traditional Dora Milaje spear.

REBEL SPIRIT

Aneka may be in the Dora Milaje, but she's willing to buck tradition and give new ideas a try. She's steadfast, too, refusing to evacuate her home after Namor's attack. This Midnight Angel is truly loyal and courageous.

PROUD

Aneka is honored to be a protector of Wakanda. Okoye invites her to join her as a Midnight Angel to take on the Talokanil. As the Wakandans make their last stand, Aneka vows to take as many of their opponents as possible along with them to join the ancestors.

Golden statement earrings

Lightweight fabric shirt for warm Wakandan climate

DATA FILE

AFFILIATION: Wakanda, Dora Milaje, Shuri, Ayo
KEY STRENGTHS: Highly trained in hand-to-hand combat, melee weapons, infiltration, tactics
APPEARANCES: BP:WF

Developed by Shuri and her response team, the advanced Midnight Angel suit is a feat of technology. It gives Aneka the ability to fly, as well as superhuman strength, speed, and durability.

NAMOR

Imperius Rex

The charismatic leader of Talokan has many names. His people call him K'uk'ulkan; his enemies know him as Namor. When Wakanda reveals the power of vibranium to the world, Namor is furious. He believes that the search for more vibranium will lead other nations to discover his people and their source of the metal.

Beaded mantle with snake design

Vibranium spear with jade accents

Vibranium bracers withstand most weapons

Vibranium belt

Vibranium shin guards

Pair of feathery wings on each ankle

DATA FILE

AFFILIATION: Talokan
KEY STRENGTHS: Enhanced strength, speed, agility, and durability, slowed aging, ability to breathe on land and in water, flight
APPEARANCES: BP:WF

MAJESTY

Namor's mother and her Yucatán village were overwhelmed by conquerors. To escape, they chose to undergo a metamorphosis that let them draw oxygen from the ocean. Later, Namor became ruler of their new underwater kingdom.

ONE OF A KIND

Namor's mother was still pregnant with him when she underwent the metamorphosis. Due to its effects, Namor was born unique, with pointed ears, wings on his ankles, and the ability to breathe in both air and water.

When Wakanda will not side with Talokan against the world, Namor declares war. He attacks the country's capital and fights its guardian, the Black Panther.

NAMORA

Fierce leader

Namora is a high-ranking Talokanil leader who will do whatever it takes to protect the people of her underwater kingdom. Tough, straightforward, and a powerful warrior, she wields a barbed spear. Namora often advises Namor and encourages him to act against Wakanda before it's too late.

Lionfish fin hair adornment

Breathing mask

Striped lionfish fins embellish Namora's headdress and armor. She attacks Ironheart with the ferocity of the fish's namesake.

Golden coral-like jewelry

Textiles handmade from underwater materials

IN CHARGE

Namora orders Attuma and the other warriors of Talokan to wipe out Riri Williams and her Wakandan protectors. After Shuri appeals to Namora in her own language, she agrees to let them speak to Namor.

SAFE AT LAST

Hundreds of years ago, Namora's people gained the ability to breathe underwater after eating a blue plant growing in the sea. They built a new life in the ocean, away from human war and disease.

DATA FILE

AFFILIATION: Talokan, Namor
KEY STRENGTHS: Underwater breathing, superhuman strength, durability, and swim speed, trained warrior
APPEARANCES: BP:WF

ATTUMA

Water warrior

Very few fighters can go toe to toe with Okoye of the Dora Milaje. Attuma is one of them. He's powerful even among the resilient people of Talokan. As Attuma and Okoye battle, a swing of his axe sends Okoye sliding back several feet, and he quickly overpowers her.

Headpiece made from skull and jawbones

HAMMERHEAD
Attuma wears the skull of a hammerhead shark as a headpiece. Shark teeth also adorn his armor, which protects him from his foes' bullets and other piercing attacks.

Breathing mask

In or out of water, Attuma is a force to be reckoned with. He follows orders to attack without hesitation.

Vibranium-blade spear adorned with teeth

Handcrafted gold belt decoration

CONTEMPT
Attuma has absolutely no respect for humans. During their battle, he taunts Okoye by kicking her spear back to her. When Okoye falls to the ground, he tells her that she's not worth his blade.

DATA FILE
AFFILIATION: Talokan, Namor, Namora
KEY STRENGTHS: Underwater breathing, superhuman strength, durability, and swim speed, hand-to-hand combat
APPEARANCES: BP:WF

RIRI WILLIAMS

Ironheart

Riri Williams is a brilliant student at an elite college. She builds a machine that can detect vibranium. As a result, nations around the world seek out the 19-year-old scientist. But Riri has been working on other projects, too ...

Goggles protect from high winds

Over-the-shoulder harness

Engines of Riri's own design

GIFTED

Riri started building machines when she was three years old. She works out of loaned garage space, where she's spent years piecing together her own advanced armor suit, inspired by Stark technology.

Heart-shaped power source

Resourceful Riri built the vibranium detector with components she found in a junkyard. She proves the skepticism of her metallurgy professor is misplaced.

MARK II

With Wakandan technology and materials at her disposal, Riri has given her second Ironheart armor a sleeker design and significant upgrades. It is more maneuverable and capable of moving at higher speeds.

Boosters controlled by hand

Joints uncovered for ease of movement

Fires energy blasts

Scrounged machinery parts

Thick rubber soles for impact on landing

DATA FILE

AFFILIATION: Shuri, Ramonda, Okoye
KEY STRENGTHS: Genius inventor and scientific mind; as Ironheart: flight, enhanced strength, speed, and durability, advanced weaponry
APPEARANCES: BP:WF

JENTORRA

Revolutionary warrior

THINKING AHEAD

Jentorra isn't a hotheaded warrior who jumps into battle without thought. She's a wise leader who meditates and spends time carefully thinking of her next move. She's always ready with a plan when it's time to act.

Helmet and armor made from creature bones

Pauldron protects nonweapon arm

Plates protect joints

Holstered energy weapon

Sharp-tipped staff

Deep in the Quantum Realm, Jentorra and her ragtag group of freedom fighters rebel against Kang. He burned their homes and built his citadel on the ashes. His power is so great that the rebels don't expect to win the battle, but Jentorra keeps fighting. When she meets outsiders from the world above, she realizes they've led Kang's forces straight to her camp.

AMBUSH

Jentorra overhears Scott Lang say the name "Janet." She knows Kang will be looking for anyone associated with Janet Van Dyne and orders an immediate evacuation. Ships on the horizon confirm her fears. Jentorra and the other rebels fight back, but they're outmatched by Kang's heavily armored Quantumnauts.

Cassie Lang frees the rebel leader from Kang's detention cell. Cassie and Jentorra work together to broadcast an inspiring message of rebellion and free the other prisoners.

DATA FILE

AFFILIATION: Quantum Realm, Quaz, Veb, Xolum
KEY STRENGTHS: Trained in combat, strategy, leadership
APPEARANCES: AMATW:Q

QUAZ

Tired telepath

Quaz is a freedom fighter in the Quantum Realm. He has the ability to read minds, which usually ends up giving him way more information than he wants or needs. Quaz is a talented telepath, however, and can quickly access the thoughts he's looking for when the moment calls for it. When Quaz uses telepathy, his forehead glows and emits a distinct ringing sound.

REBELLION

Quaz might be more of a thinker, but he fights just as hard as any of the other rebels. After Jentorra rallies the freedom fighters for one last decisive battle against Kang, he rushes toward the Quantumnauts at her side.

Quaz meets Scott and Cassie Lang in the Quantum Realm. His job is to make sure they're not spies. He hears the words "San Francisco" and "Earth" in their thoughts but doesn't know what they mean.

Robe with handpainted runes

Bone necklace

TOO MUCH KNOWLEDGE

There are many times Quaz wishes that he couldn't hear other people's thoughts. No matter how hard he tries, Scott can't stop thinking impolite things about Quaz's glowing forehead.

DATA FILE

AFFILIATION: Quantum Realm, Jentorra, Veb
KEY STRENGTHS: Telepathy, loyalty, bravery
APPEARANCES: AMATW:Q

VEB

Freedom fighter

Friendly Veb is a resident of the Quantum Realm and part of the rebellion against Kang. He's an invaluable member of the diverse group because the red ooze he produces, when consumed, makes all languages understandable.

Veb's warm and curious nature is a bit disconcerting for Scott Lang. He's delighted when Scott drinks his ooze and is able to understand him.

Thought process center and visual organs

INTO BATTLE

Jentorra calls the charge and Veb runs full speed ahead. He's an easy target for the Quantumnauts waiting to ambush the rebels. Their energy weapons blast him full of holes ... and Veb is overjoyed. He forcefully sucks in air through the new holes, along with some unlucky Quantumnauts.

Body composed of unknown quantum substance

Holes

Tentacle-like appendages emit edible ooze

DATA FILE

AFFILIATION: Quantum Realm, Jentorra, Quaz, Xolum
KEY STRENGTHS: Secretes an ooze that translates all spoken words when consumed, holes in body pull in air and objects, regeneration, good hugs
APPEARANCES: AMATW:Q

More holes

HUGGER

It doesn't take long for Veb to consider someone a friend. After Kang's defeat, Veb thanks Cassie Lang and gives her a heartfelt hug goodbye. Cassie is surprised and delighted.

ADAM WARLOCK

Golden child

Adam is the pinnacle of the Sovereign people. Although he wields great power granted by genetic manipulation, Adam is still childlike and immature. He ventures into the galaxy with his mother Ayesha on a mission to save their people. The High Evolutionary threatens to wipe out the entire Sovereign civilization if they don't find experiment 89P13, also known as Rocket.

Golden hair of the Sovereign

Adam gets annoyed with his mother ordering him around, but he loves her dearly. Ayesha is still on board their ship when it's destroyed by the High Evolutionary.

Golden pauldrons

A SECOND CHANCE

Adam Warlock finds Groot on board the High Evolutionary's ship and prepares to fight—and then faints from his injuries. Groot gets him to safety, much to Adam's surprise. The young Sovereign has a change of heart and saves Peter Quill before he runs out of air in the vacuum of space.

Red cape shows flair for the dramatic

Plated armor weak against Nebula's blade

DATA FILE

AFFILIATION: The Sovereign, Ayesha, Guardians of the Galaxy
KEY STRENGTHS: Superhuman strength, agility, and durability, energy blasts, flight, survival in space
APPEARANCES: GOTGV3

THE HIGH EVOLUTIONARY

Merciless scientist

The High Evolutionary seeks to create a perfect world. He relentlessly pursues the creation of a highly intelligent and peaceful people by cobbling together species gathered across the galaxy. His methods are cruel and inhumane, and he disposes of the creatures he creates without a second thought. Only one of the High Evolutionary's experiments, 89P13, demonstrates the exceptional qualities he's searching for. 89P13 later chooses a new name: Rocket.

Recorder Vim and Recorder Theel work for the High Evolutionary faithfully, until his mission to reclaim Rocket endangers their ship, the *Arête*. Vim turns on her leader, but her victory is short-lived.

MISGUIDED GENIUS

The High Evolutionary sees himself as a good guy, not a conqueror. He thinks that no cost is too high if the end result is the betterment of the universe. He is ready to destroy entire worlds and their millions of inhabitants in his desire for "perfection."

Technologically advanced body armor

Hand focuses gravity manipulation

Long purple robes made of expensive material

LESSON LEARNED

After suffering severe injuries at the hands of Rocket, the High Evolutionary wears protective armor and turns his transformative experiments on himself. He gains the ability to control gravity. He effortlessly moves large pieces of debris and immobilizes Star-Lord and Groot with just a gesture.

DATA FILE

AFFILIATION: OrgoCorp, Counter-Earth, Recorder Theel, Recorder Vim
KEY STRENGTHS: Genius-level intellect, accelerates evolution through technology, vast wealth and resources, gravity manipulation
APPEARANCES: GOTGV3

INDEX

Page numbers in **bold** refer to main entries.

Fontaine, Contessa Valentina Allegra de 161, **163**, 168
Foster, Dr. Bill 133, **134**
Foster, Dr. Jane **21**, 23, 28, 29, 57
Frigga 19, 20, 22, **23**
Frost Giants 20, 23, 27
Fury, Nick 10, **12**, 48, 59, 141, 145
  and Carol Danvers 12, 137, 142

G

Gamora 47, 49, 62, **63**, 65, 68, 69, 105, 108
  2014 Gamora 148, **149**
Gap Junction 202
Ghost *see* Starr, Ava
G'iah 145
Gilgamesh **185**, 193
Glaive, Corvus **130**, 131
Golden Daggers Club 15, 178
Goose **142**
Gorr the God Butcher 24, 115
the Grandmaster 109, 110, **113**, 114
the Great Protector 176, 179
Groot (original) 64, **65**, 102
Groot (younger) 65, **102**, 232, 233
Guardians of the Galaxy 62, 65, 66, 107, 108, 218
  see also individual members

H

Habooska the Horrible 217, **218**
Hammer, Justin 6, 7, **17**
Hammer Industries 7, 17
Hansen, Maya 51, **52**
Harkness, Agatha 74, **153**, 158
Hawkeye *see* Barton, Clint
Heimdall **25**, 112
Hela 19, 20, 22, 110, **111**, 112, 117
Helicarrier 10, 12, 48
the High Evolutionary 64, 102, 104, 107, 232, **233**
Hill, Maria 12, **48**
Ho, Dr. Yinsen **11**
Hogan, Harold "Happy" **7**, 53

Howling Commandos 37, 39, 40, 41, 45
  see also individual members
Hulk *see* Banner, Dr. Bruce
Hunter B-15 **167**
Hydra 12, 35, 43, 45, 73, 74, 171
  and Bucky Barnes 34, 37
  and Dr. Arnim Zola 42
  and Jasper Sitwell 32
  and S.H.I.E.L.D. 48, 59
  and Steve Rogers (Captain America) 33, 34, 40, 58

I

Ikaris 183, **184**, 186, 187, 189, 190
The Illuminati 203, 204, 205
Incursion 207, 208
Indigarr 217, 218
Infinity Gauntlet 77, 128
Infinity Stones 4, 13, 42, 57, 65, 68, 81
  Mind Stone 20, 74, 76, 77, 130, 131
  Soul Stone 35, 63, 69
  Space Stone 130, 140, 147
  and Thanos 47, 94, 95, 119, 128, 129, 130, 131, 137, 147, 148, 149
  Time Stone 95, 97, 104, 129, 132
Iron Gang 177
Iron Legion 76
Iron Man *see* Stark, Tony
Iron Monger *see* Stane, Obadiah
Iron Patriot 50, **55**
Ironheart *see* Williams, Riri

J

Jabari Tribe 121, 126
Jentorra **229**, 230, 231
Jones, Gabe **38**
Jotunheim 26, 27

K

Kaecilius 96, 97, 98, 99, **100**, 101

Kamran **216**
Kang 7, 80, 85, 86, 229, 230, 231
Katy **175**
Keener, Harley **56**
Khan, Aamir **214**
Khan, Kamala (Ms. Marvel) **209**, 210, 211, 214, 215, 216
Khan, Muneeba **214**, **215**
Khan, Yusuf 211, **214**, **215**
Khan family 211, **214–15**
Killian, Aldrich 5, 50, **51**, 52, 53, 54, 55
Killmonger, Erik 91, 93, **120**, 125
  and Okoye 118
  and Princess Shuri 119
  and T'Challa 92, 119, 120, 121, 122, 124, 126, 127
Kingo 182, **190**, 191
Kingpin *see* Fisk, Wilson
Klaue, Ulysses 93, 120, 122, 124, **125**
Knowhere 47, 66, 69, 71, 72
Korath 68, **70**, 143
Korg **115**, 116
Kraglin **71**, 72, 106
Krec 67, 68, **70**, 138, 139, 145
  Kree-Skrull War 70
Kro **193**
Kruger, Heinz 36, **43**
the Kyln 64, 65, 66

L

Lang, Cassie 80, 85, **87**, 88, 229, 230, 231
Lang, Maggie 87, 88
Lang, Scott (Ant-Man) 7, **80**, 231
  and Ant-Thony 89
  and Cassie Lang 80, 87, 230
  and Hank Pym 80, 81, 84, 88
  and Janet Van Dyne 86, 229
  and Jimmy Woo 135
  in the Quantum Realm 80, 86, 87, 230, 231
  and Yellowjacket 85
Laufey, King 20, **27**
Lawson, Dr. Wendy 140, 141
Lewis, Dr. Darcy 28, **29**, 30, 135, 146
Li 176, **177**, 179
Loki 10, **20**, 21, 78

and the Chitauri 49
and Dr. Erik Selvig 28
and Frigga 20, 23
L1130 variant 164, 165, 166, 167
and Laufey 20, 27
Loki (TVA) **152**
and Odin 20, 22
and Thor 19, 20
Lopez, Maya **197**, 198
Lucky the Pizza Dog **196**

M

Makkari 188, **189**, 193, 194
Malekith 20, 21, 23, 30, **57**
the Mandarin *see* Slattery, Trevor
Mantis 66, **104**, 108
Mar-Vell **140**, 145
Martinex **105**
Marvel, Captain *see* Danvers, Carol
Mason, Rick **173**
Maw, Ebony 4, **129**, 132
Maximoff, Billy **156**, 157, 204
Maximoff, Pietro **73**, 74, 157, 158
Maximoff, Tommy 156, **157**, 204
Maximoff, Wanda (The Scarlet Witch) **74**, 98, 158, 203, 205
  838-Wanda Maximoff **204**
  and Agatha Harkness 74, 153, 158
  and America Chavez 74, 201
  Chaos Magic 74, 153, 156, 157, 158
  and Dr. Darcy Lewis 29
  and Monica Rambeau 146
  and Pietro 73, 74
  and Vision 77, 130, 131, 154, 155, 156, 157
M'Baku **126**
Melina **170**
Midnight, Proxima **131**
Midnight Angels 118
Miek 115, **116**
The Mighty Thor *see* Foster, Dr. Jane
Mind Stone 20, 74, 76, 77, 130, 131
Minn-Erva **144**

DK would like to thank Kevin Feige, Louis D'Esposito, Brad Winderbaum, Jacqueline Ryan-Rudolph, Capri Ciulla, Nigel Goodwin, Erika Denton, Jennifer Wojnar, Jeff Willis, Jennifer Giandalone, Vince Garcia, Sarah Truly Beers, and Kristy Amornkul at Marvel Studios; Caitlin O'Connell and Jeff Youngquist at Marvel; and Chelsea Alon, Elana Cohen, Stephanie Everett, Kurt Hartman, and John Morgan III at Disney. DK would also like to thank Julia March for editorial assistance; Vanessa Bird for the index; and Vicky Armstrong, Simon Beecroft, Megan Douglass, Julie Ferris, Emma Grange, Lisa Lanzarini, Shari Last, David McDonald, Helen Peters, Cefn Ridout, Sadie Smith, Marc Staples, Jess Tapolcai, and Jonathan Wakeham for their work on the previous edition of this book.

AVAILABLE NOW ON VARIOUS FORMATS INCLUDING DIGITAL
WHERE APPLICABLE FOR THE FOLLOWING FILMS AND DISNEY+ ORIGINAL SERIES:
Iron Man, The Incredible Hulk, Iron Man 2, Thor, Captain America: The First Avenger, Marvel's The Avengers, Iron Man 3, Thor: The Dark World, Captain America: The Winter Soldier, Guardians Of The Galaxy, Avengers: Age Of Ultron, Ant-Man, Captain America: Civil War, Doctor Strange, Guardians Of The Galaxy Vol. 2, Thor: Ragnarok, Black Panther, Avengers: Infinity War, Ant-Man And The Wasp, Captain Marvel, Avengers: Endgame, WandaVision, The Falcon And The Winter Soldier, Loki, Black Widow, Shang-Chi And The Legend Of The Ten Rings, Eternals, Hawkeye, Doctor Strange In The Multiverse Of Madness, Ms. Marvel, Thor: Love And Thunder, She-Hulk: Attorney At Law, Black Panther: Wakanda Forever, Ant-Man And The Wasp: Quantumania, Guardians Of The Galaxy Vol. 3, The Marvels
© 2024 MARVEL

Senior Editor Ruth Amos
Senior Designer Nathan Martin
US Senior Editor Jennette ElNaggar
Jacket design by Mark Penfound
Senior Production Editor Jennifer Murray
Senior Production Controller Mary Slater
Managing Editor Rachel Lawrence
Managing Art Editor Vicky Short
Publishing Director Mark Searle

Designed for DK by Robert Perry

This American Edition, 2024
First American Edition, 2019
Published in the United States by DK Publishing
1745 Broadway, 20th Floor, New York, NY 10019

Page design copyright © 2024 Dorling Kindersley Limited
DK, a Division of Penguin Random House LLC
24 25 26 27 28 10 9 8 7 6 5 4 3 2 1
001–338654–April/2024

© 2024 MARVEL

All rights reserved.
Without limiting the rights under the copyright reserved above, no part of this publication may be reproduced, stored in or introduced into a retrieval system, or transmitted, in any form, or by any means (electronic, mechanical, photocopying, recording, or otherwise), without the prior written permission of the copyright owner.
Published in Great Britain by Dorling Kindersley Limited

A catalog record for this book is available from the Library of Congress.
ISBN 978-0-7440-9263-9

DK books are available at special discounts when purchased in bulk for sales promotions, premiums, fund-raising, or educational use.
For details, contact: DK Publishing Special Markets, 1745 Broadway, 20th Floor, New York, NY 10019
SpecialSales@dk.com

Printed and bound in China

www.dk.com
www.marvel.com

MIX
Paper | Supporting responsible forestry
FSC™ C018179

This book was made with Forest Stewardship Council™ certified paper – one small step in DK's commitment to a sustainable future.
Learn more at www.dk.com/uk/information/sustainability